"You'll need both hands for this."

"When you swing the ax back, let your right one slip up the handle. But whatever you do, always hold on hard with your left, like this. Want to try?" he asked.

When she took the ax, her fingers brushed over his.

Rye stepped back and reached around Lisa until his hands were positioned above and below hers on the long handle. Every time she breathed in, a blend of evergreen resin and warmth and man filled her senses. His skin was smooth against hers, hot, and the hair on his arms glistened beneath the sun in shades of sable and bronze.

With each motion Rye made, his chest brushed against Lisa's back, telling her that barely a breath separated their bodies.

"Lisa?"

Helplessly she looked over her shoulder at Rye. His mouth was only inches away.

"Come closer," he whispered, bending down to her. "Closer. Yes, like that."

ELIZABETH LOWELL
FEVER

MIRA BOOKS

ISBN 1-55166-314-7

FEVER

To Francis Ray,
salt of the earth
and sweetness, too

1

Ryan McCall climbed out of the battered ranch pickup and instantly began unbuttoning his city shirt. He had flown from Texas to a small local landing strip in Utah where he kept one of the few luxuries he had bought for himself—a plane that could get him in and out of his father's life in nothing flat. From the airstrip he had driven in the pickup over increasingly primitive roads until he reached his home in the early afternoon. He had loved every rough inch of the way, because each rock and rut meant that he was farther removed from the father he loved and could not get along with for more than a few minutes at a time.

"It was worth it, though," Rye told himself aloud as he stretched his long, powerful arms over his head. "That Angus bull of his is just what my herd needs."

Unfortunately it had taken Rye two weeks to

convince Edward McCall II that his son would not, repeat *not*, marry some useless Houston belle just to get his hands on the Angus bull. Once that was understood, the negotiations for the bull had gone quickly.

Rye turned his face up to the afternoon sun and smiled with sensual pleasure at the warmth pouring over him. The Texas sun had been hot. Too hot. He preferred the golden heat of Utah's mountain country, where the lowland's fierce sun was gentled by altitude and winds smelling of piñon and distant pines. The air was dry, brilliant in its clarity, and the small river that wound through the Rocking M was a cool, glittering rush of blue.

Eyes closed, shirt undone, Rye stood and let the peace he always felt on his own land steal over him. It had been a long two weeks. His father had just turned sixty. His lack of grandsons to carry on the family name had been duly noted—about six times an hour. Even his sister, who was normally a staunch ally, had told him sweetly that she would be bringing up a very special girl for the end-of-the-summer dance Rye always held at his ranch. Rye had ignored his sister, but he hadn't been able to ignore the endless stream of moist-lipped debutantes or accomplished divorcées who were trembling with eagerness to get their perfectly manicured claws into the McCall pocketbook.

Rye's mouth shifted into a sardonic smile. He could afford to be amused by the women's transparent greed now; he was home, beyond their reach, and he thanked God for every instant of his freedom. Whistling softly, he pulled out his shirttails and leaped onto the porch without touching any of the three steps. The movement was catlike in its speed, grace and precision.

Since Rye had come into his mother's small inheritance at twenty-one, he had spent his time digging postholes, felling trees and riding thousands of miles over his own ranch. The hard labor showed in his powerful body. The lithe flex and play of muscles beneath tanned skin had attracted more than one feminine glance. Rye discounted his appearance as any part of the reason women lined up at his door, however. He had seen his father and his younger brother fall prey to too many greedy women to believe that any woman would want him for any reason other than his bank account, which meant that he had very little use for women at all.

The instant Rye walked into his house, he knew that someone else was there. The room smelled of perfume rather than the sunshine and fresh air that he preferred. He turned and saw a woman standing in the dining room. She had pulled open a sideboard drawer and was looking at its utilitarian contents with a combination of curiosity and disbelief.

"Taking inventory?" Rye asked coolly.

The woman made a startled sound and spun to face him. The movement sent black hair flying. There was no shifting of cloth, however; the clothes she was wearing were too tight to float with any movement she made. Big, dark eyes took in every detail of Rye's appearance. They widened at the breadth of his shoulders and the thick mat of hair that began at his collarbone and disappeared beneath the narrow waist of his pants. The speculation in the woman's eyes increased as she approvingly inspected the fit of his slacks.

A single fast look told Rye that his father had gone all out this time. The woman was built like a particularly lush hourglass and had paid a tailor to prove it. Not a single ripe curve went unannounced. The blouse was too well made to strain at the buttons with each breath she took, but it was a near thing. Automatically Rye put her in the "experienced divorcée" category.

"Hello," she said, holding out her hand to him and smiling. "My name's Cherry Larson."

"Goodbye, Cherry Larson. Tell Dad you tried, but I threw you out so hard you bounced. He might feel sorry enough for you to buy you a trinket." Rye's words were clipped, as cold as the gray eyes staring through Cherry, dismissing her as he turned away.

"Dad?"

"Edward McCall II," Rye said, heading for the staircase, pulling off his shirt. "The Texan who paid you to seduce me."

"Oh." She frowned. "He told you?"

"He didn't have to. Overblown brunettes are his style, not mine."

The bedroom door slammed, leaving Cherry Larson to examine the stainless steel flatware in peace.

A few moments later Rye emerged in boots, Levi's and work shirt. Cherry was still standing in the dining room. He passed her without a look, lifted his hat from a peg by the kitchen door and said, "I'm going for a ride. When I get back, you won't be here."

"But—but how will I get into town?"

"Wait around for a silver-haired cowboy called Lassiter. He loves taking women like you for a ride."

Rye walked to the barn with long, angry strides. The first thing he saw was Devil, his favorite mount. The big horse was tied to the corral fence, swishing flies with a long, black tail. Saddled, bridled, ready to go.

Instantly Rye knew that at least one of the cowhands had realized how he would react when he saw the woman lying in wait for him in his own home. He'd bet that the thoughtful cowhand had been Jim. He was happily married, yet he fully sympathized with his boss's desire to stay single.

"Jim, you just earned yourself a bonus," Rye muttered as he untied the reins and swung onto the big black horse.

Devil bunched his powerful haunches and tugged impatiently at the bit, demanding a run. He hadn't been ridden by anyone during the weeks that Rye had been gone, and Devil was a horse that had been born to run.

There was no one in sight as Rye cantered out past the barn. For a moment he wondered about the fact that none of his men had turned out to say hello, then he realized that the hands were probably back in the barn somewhere, laughing at his reaction to the lushly baited trap set in his lair. The men could have warned him about Cherry's presence, but that would have spoiled the joke, and there was nothing a cowboy loved better than a joke—no matter who it was on. So they had just made themselves scarce until the fun was over.

Reluctantly Rye smiled, then laughed out loud. He spun the big horse on its hocks just in time to see several men filing out of the barn. Rye waved his dark hat in a big arc before spinning Devil around again and giving the horse the freedom to run that it had been begging for.

As the trail to McCall's Meadow glided by under Devil's long stride, Rye relaxed again, relishing his freedom. The high, small meadow was his favorite part of the ranch, his ultimate retreat from the frustrations of being Edward Ryan McCall III. Usually he was one of the first people to reach the mountain meadow after the snow melted in the pass, but the melt had come very late this year. He hadn't had time to get to the meadow before he had gone to Houston to negotiate for the purchase of one of his father's prize bulls.

Before Rye had bought the ranch, the various high meadows had been used as summer pasture for cattle and sheep. Most of the meadows still pastured cattle. The small, high bowl that had come to be called McCall's Meadow hadn't been touched for ten years. Dr. Thompson had been very eloquent in his plea that Rye, as one of the few ranchers who could afford it, should be the one to lead the way in allowing a small part of his land to return to what it had been before white men had come to the West. The resulting patterns of regrowth in the plants and the return of native animals would be studied in detail, and what was learned would be used to help reclaim other lands from overgrazing.

In truth, Rye hadn't needed much persuading to participate in Dr. Thompson's study. Rye might have been born in the city but he had never loved it. He loved the rugged land, though. He loved riding through sunlight and wind and silence, and

seeing mountains rise above him, their flanks a
magnificent patchwork of evergreen forest, blue-
gray sage and quaking aspen that turned from
green to shimmering silver under a caressing
breeze. The land gave him peace.

And if a man took care of the land, unlike a
woman, the land would take care of him in return.

That same afternoon Lisa Johansen sat by a
mountain stream and slowly trailed her fingers
through the cool, clean water. The sunlight that
smoothed over her was as warm and sensual as
her daydream, making a languid heat uncurl deep
within her as she stretched to meet her dream. *He
will be like the mountains, strong and rugged and
enduring. He will look at me and see not a pale
outsider but the woman of his dreams. He will
smile and hold out his hand and then he'll gather
me in his arms and...*

Whether she was awake or asleep, the dream
always ended there. Wryly Lisa acknowledged to
herself that it was just as well; she had a thorough
intellectual understanding of what came next, but
her practical experience in a man's arms was one
zero followed by another and another, world without end, amen. Isolation from her peers had been
the biggest drawback to the kind of life she had
led with her parents, who were anthropologists.
There had always been men about, but none of

them were for her. They had been tribal men who were cultural light-years apart from herself and her parents.

With a sigh Lisa scooped up a palmful of water and drank, letting the shimmering coolness spread through her. After two weeks, she still didn't take for granted the mountain water flowing clean and sweet and pure, day and night, a liquid miracle always within her reach. As she bent to drink again, the muted sound of hoofbeats came to her.

Lisa straightened and shaded her eyes with her hand. At the entrance to the high, small valley were two riders. She stood up, wiped her dripping hand on her worn jeans and mentally reviewed her meager supplies. When she had taken the job of watching over McCall's Meadow through the brief, high-country summer, she hadn't realized that she would need to buy so many supplies from her tiny food budget. But then, she hadn't realized that Boss Mac's cowboys would be such frequent visitors to the meadow. Since she had first met the cowboys ten days ago, they had been back almost every day, swearing that nobody made pan bread and bacon like she did.

The shorter of the two cowboys took off his hat and waved it in a wide arc. Lisa waved back, recognizing Lassiter, Boss Mac's foreman. The man with him was Jim. If they had other names, the men hadn't mentioned them and she would never ask. In many of the primitive tribes among which she had been raised, to ask someone for his full name—or for any name at all—was unspeakably rude.

"Morning, Miss Lisa," Lassiter said, dismounting from his horse. "How're them seeds doing? They slipped through that old fence and flown away yet?"

Lisa smiled and shook her head. Ever since she had told Lassiter that she was here to watch the grass seeds growing within the big meadow fence, he had teased her about runaway seeds that needed to be "hog-tied and throwed 'fore they learned their rightful place."

"I haven't lost any seeds yet," Lisa said gravely, "but I'm being real careful, just like you told me. I'm particularly watchful when the moon is up. That's when all sorts of odd things take a notion to fly."

Lassiter heard Lisa's precise echoes of his earlier deadpan warnings and knew that she was gently pulling his leg. He laughed and slapped his hat against his jeans, releasing a small puff of trail dust that was almost as silver as his hair. "You'll do, Miss Lisa. You'll do just fine. Boss Mac won't find one seed missing when he gets back from Houston. Good thing, too. He's hell on wheels after a few weeks of having his pa parade eager fillies past him."

Lisa smiled rather sadly. She knew what it was like to disagree with parents on the subject of marriage. Her parents had wanted to her to marry a man like themselves, a scholar with a taste for adventure. So they had sent her to the United States and their old friend Professor Thompson with instructions to find her a suitable mate. Lisa had come, but not to find a husband. She had come to see if the United States would be her home, if she would finally find a place that would hold the answer to the hot restlessness that burned like a fever in her dreams, in her blood.

"Hello, Miss Lisa," the second man said, climbing down and standing almost shyly to the side. "This here mountain must agree with you. You're pretty as a daisy."

"Thank you," Lisa said, smiling quickly at the lanky cowhand. "How's the baby? Has he cut that tooth yet?"

Jim sighed. "Durn thing's stubborn as a stump. He keeps a-chewin' and a-chewin' and nothin' happens. But the missus says to thank you. She tried rubbing that oil you gave her on the gum and the baby was right soothed."

The smile on Lisa's face widened. Some things didn't change, no matter the culture nor the country. Oil of cloves was an ancient remedy for gum troubles, yet it had been all but forgotten in America. It pleased Lisa that something she had learned half a world and cultural centuries distant from Utah's mountains could help the fat-cheeked baby whose picture Jim proudly displayed at every opportunity.

"You and Lassiter are just in time for lunch," Lisa said. "Why don't you water your horses while I build up the fire?"

As one, Lassiter and Jim turned toward their mounts. Instead of leading the animals away, both men untied gunnysacks that had been secured behind the saddles.

"The missus said you must be getting right tired of bread and beans and bacon," Jim said, holding out a sack. "Thought you might like some cookies and things for a change."

Before Lisa could thank him, Lassiter held out two bulging sacks. "Cook said he had more food hanging around than he could set fire to 'fore it went bad. You'd be doing us a favor if you took it off our hands."

For a moment Lisa could say nothing. Then she blinked against the stinging in her eyes and thanked both men. It was very comforting to know that generosity, like a baby's first tooth, was a part of human experience everywhere in the world.

While the men watered their horses, Lisa added a few more sticks to the fire from her dwindling supply of wood, mixed up a batch of dough and checked the soot-blackened kettle that served as a coffeepot. To her joy, a generous supply of coffee had been included in the supplies that the men had packed up the trail for her. There was also dried and fresh fruit, more flour, dried beef, fresh beef, rice, salt, oil and other packages she didn't have time to investigate before the men came back from the stream. The sacks were a treasure trove to Lisa, who had been accustomed to seeing food measured out carefully except for the rare feast days.

Humming happily, Lisa planned meals that would have been impossible before Lassiter and Jim had come riding up the trail with their generous gifts. She had come to America with almost no cash. If there had been any money left over from the grants that supported her parents, it had always gone to help out the desperately poor among the natives. Nor did the job of being caretaker in McCall's Meadow pay anything beyond a roof over her head, a fixed amount of money for supplies and a stipend so small it could only be called an allowance.

The cabin itself was ancient. Previous students had joked that it had been built by God just after He finished the mountains surrounding it. There was a hearth, walls, floor, roof and not much else. The lack of electricity, running water and other such amenities didn't bother Lisa. She would have loved to have some of the beautiful carpets that the Bedouin tribes used to brighten and soften their austere lives, but she was more than content with the gentle sun, clean air, abundant water and near absence of flies. To her, those things were true luxuries.

And if she wanted to touch something soft and exquisitely made, she had only to open up her pack and admire her parents' parting gift to her. The yards of cloth were a linen so fine that it felt like silk. One piece was a luminous dove gray meant to be made into a swirling dress. The other piece was a glowing amethyst that was the exact color of her eyes. It, too, was destined to be made into a dress.

Despite their alluring beauty, Lisa hadn't cut into either length of cloth. She knew that they were meant to help her find a husband. She didn't want that. She wanted more from life than a man who saw her as a cross between a producer of sons and a beast of burden. Few of the native marriages Lisa had seen aroused in her anything but a mixed admiration for the women's stamina. Intellectually she knew why the nubile girls her age and younger had watched men with dark, speculative eyes and measuring smiles. Emotionally Lisa had never felt the strange fever that she had seen burning in other girls' blood, making them forget the lessons of their mothers and grandmothers, aunts and sisters.

Secretly that was what Lisa had always hoped to find somewhere in the world—the fever that burned through body and mind, the fever that burned all the way through to the soul. Yet she had never felt farther away from it than in America, where the boys her own age seemed very young, full of laughter and untested confidence, untouched by famine and death. During the few days that she had lived with Professor Thompson, waiting for the pass into McCall's Meadow to open, she had met many students; but not once had she looked at the males around her with ancient female curiosity in her eyes and fever rising in her blood.

She had begun to doubt that she ever would.

2

"Sure smells good," Lassiter said, coming up behind Lisa as she cooked. "You know, you're the only one of Professor Thompson's kids we haven't had to teach how to make real camp coffee."

"In Morocco, coffee isn't coffee until it's so thick it barely pours," Lisa said.

"Yeah? You'll have to make that for me someday."

"Bring lots of tinned milk, then. And sugar."

"Think so?"

She nodded.

"Real horseshoe floater, huh?"

Lisa hadn't heard the phrase before. The image it conjured in her mind made her laugh. "Actually, it would probably float the horse, too."

Chuckling, Lassiter looked around the camp, approving of the order that Lisa had brought to the area. Twigs for kindling and thicker sticks for burning had been stacked within easy reach of the campfire, along with a few larger pieces of wood. The ground itself had been recently swept with a broom made of twigs. The various tools that had been broken or abandoned by other students had been gathered by Lisa and laid out neatly on a log. The tools ranged in size from a slender awl to a battered wedge and sledgehammer used for splitting logs. The big, double-edged logger's ax that came with the cabin showed recent signs of having been sharpened, although Lassiter couldn't imagine what Lisa had used to hone it. Nor could he imagine her using the ax itself. The handle was four feet long, and she was only a few inches over five feet.

The ax reminded Lassiter that he had meant to see how Lisa was fixed for firewood. Unlike the other students, she cooked her food over a campfire rather than on a camp stove. Lassiter suspected that she didn't even have such a stove. In fact, he suspected that she didn't have much at all beyond the clothes she stood in and the bedroll that was being aired right now over a small bush. Yet despite her obvious lack of money, she had never begrudged him or any of the McCall cowhands a meal, regardless of how many men there were or how often they showed up. She had always offered food no matter what the time of day, as though she knew what it meant to be hungry and didn't want anyone to leave her camp with an empty belly.

"Jim, why don't you and me snake a few logs on down here," Lassiter said, settling his hat on his head firmly. "We won't have time to cut them up today, but we can get them ready. Twigs and sticks are all well and good, but a proper fire needs proper wood."

"You don't have to," Lisa began. "I can—"

"Durn things are blocking the trail," Jim interrupted, mumbling. He snagged the heavy ax in one hand and turned to his horse. "Boss Mac would have our hides if a horse tripped on 'em and came up lame."

"Miss Lisa, you'd be doing us a favor just burning them up," Lassiter said firmly as he stepped into the stirrup.

Lisa looked from one man to the other, then said simply, "Thank you. I could use some more wood." As the men rode off, Lisa suddenly remembered. "Be sure that you don't take anything from inside the fence!" That was why she was here, after all. She was to protect everything behind the fence from the interference of men, so that the meadow could slowly revert to its natural state.

"Yo," Lassiter said, raising his hand in acknowledgment.

The men didn't have to go more than a hundred feet to find the kind of wood they wanted—pine logs no bigger than ten inches in diameter, the remains of trees that had fallen and had been cured through the following seasons. As Jim and Lassiter worked, preparing the logs to be dragged to the cabin, their voices carried clearly through the mountain silence.

Lisa listened to the men while she cooked, smiling from time to time at their colorful phrases when a log was especially stubborn. When the conversation shifted to the mysterious Boss Mac, she found herself holding her breath so as not to miss a word. She knew only two things about the absent owner of McCall's Meadow: his father urgently wanted Boss Mac to marry and have a son, and his men respected Boss Mac more than anything else except God.

"Then he told that redhead if'n she wanted a free ride, she should go down to the highway and wiggle her thumb," Lassiter concluded, laughing. "She was so mad she couldn't talk for a minute. Guess she thought a few nights in town with the boss meant wedding bells." The sound of the ax rang out as branches were trimmed from the log. "And then that redhead found her tongue," Lassiter continued. "Ju-das Priest! I ain't never heard such language. An' her with such a sweet smile, too."

"You get a look at the one layin' in wait for him now?" Jim asked.

He grunted with effort as the heavy ax bit into wood, making a notch for the rope to rest in while the log was dragged over to the cabin. Lassiter secured the rope around the log, then mounted his big horse and took a few turns on the rope around the saddle horn. At a touch of his heels, the horse slowly began pulling the log toward the cabin.

"Well, did you get a look?" Jim asked again as he mounted his own horse, wondering what the latest candidate for McCall's bed was like.

"Sure did." Lassiter's admiring whistle lifted musically on the mountain air. "Big dark eyes to put a deer to shame. Black hair down to her bosom—and a mighty fine bosom it was, too, all full and soft. And hips? Lordy, it was enough to make you weep. I tell you, Jim. I don't know a man alive that wouldn't want to climb into that saddle."

"Hell you don't," grunted Jim. "What about Boss Mac?"

"Oh, I wasn't talking about *marrying* it," Lassiter said. "Didn't your pa tell you? A smart man don't marry a horse just cuz he enjoys a ride now and again. Look at me."

"I'm lookin'," Jim retorted, "and I'm thinkin' most women would rather have the horse."

Lisa couldn't completely hide her laughter.

When the men heard, they realized that their conversation had carried very clearly to the camp. As they rode in, both of them looked embarrassed.

"Sorry, Miss Lisa," Jim mumbled. "Didn't mean to be sayin' such things in front of a girl."

"It's all right," she said hastily. "Really. We used to sit around the campfire and talk about Imbrihim's four wives and eight concubines and no one was embarrassed."

"Four?" Jim asked.

"Eight?" Lassiter demanded.

"For a total of twelve," Lisa agreed, grinning.

"Lor-dy," said Lassiter in admiring tones. "They make 'em strong over there, don't they?"

"Dumb," Jim muttered. "They make 'em dumb."

"Just rich," Lisa said cheerfully. "You herd cattle and Imbrihim herds camels, but things are pretty much the same underneath—in both places a strong, dumb rich man can have as many pretty, dumb women as he can afford."

Lassiter threw back his head and laughed. "You're one of a kind, Miss Lisa. But don't you go to thinking the boss is dumb. He ain't."

"That's God's truth," Jim said earnestly. "Boss Mac don't catch near as many girls as throw themselves at him. I'll bet he don't do nothing with the one waiting at the ranch now but kick her out on her high-rent keister. 'Scuse me, Miss Lisa," he added, flushing. "I forgot myself. But it's true just the same. Boss Mac is a good man and he'd be a happy one, too, if'n his pa would stop running secondhand fillies past him."

"I don't know about the one at the ranch," Lassiter said, smiling a very male smile. "Wouldn't surprise me a'tall if he kept her around. If nothing else, he needs a date for the dance, otherwise every gal in two hundred miles will be all over him like flies on fresh...er, honey."

"The dance is six weeks away," Jim protested. "He's never let a woman stay around that long."

"He's never had a woman that looked like this one," Lassiter said flatly. "She's the kind to make a man's jeans fit too tight, make no mistake about it."

Lisa made a strangled sound and nearly dropped the frying pan as a blush climbed up her fair skin at the image that came to her mind with Lassiter's words. She couldn't help wondering what it would be like to make a man burn with that kind of elemental fever. Then she remembered Lassiter's description: *Big dark eyes...black hair down to her bosom...all full and soft. And hips. Lordy!*

Glumly Lisa prodded the pan bread, knowing that the only thing a pale, slender, inexperienced blonde was likely to set fire to was lunch.

Black nostrils flared as Devil drank the wind

sweeping down out of the high country. He snorted and pulled hard at the bit. There were two trails to the meadow. One followed an old rough wagon road that had been built when the meadow was first homesteaded more than a century ago. That was the trail cattle had been driven over when the meadow was used for summer pasture. Rye could tell from the hoofprints that his men had been riding that road with unusual frequency in the past weeks. Two sets of very fresh prints told him that Lassiter's big bay and Jim's smaller cow pony had just come down out of the meadow and headed east to check on the range cattle.

The second trail hadn't been touched since the last storm. The route was precipitous, narrow, and the path all but invisible. Rye had stumbled onto it six years ago and had since used it when he was too impatient to get to the meadow's peace to take the long way around. Most horses would have balked at the path. Devil took it with the confidence of an animal born and raised in steep places.

After a long series of breathtakingly rugged switchbacks, the trail clawed up a talus slope and into a mixed grove of aspen and evergreens. The weathered cabin was just beyond the grove, at the edge of the remote meadow that was slowing reverting to its primal state. As Rye approached it, he heard the raucous cry of a whiskey jack flying through the trees and an odd series of noises that sounded rather like someone chopping wood. Rye listened for a while and then shook his head, unable to identify the sounds. The noises were too few and far between and too erratic to come from the rhythmic motions of a man chopping wood.

The horse's hooves made no sound on the bed of evergreen needles as Rye rode around the back of the cabin into the meadow. What he saw thirty feet away made him rein in the horse and shake his head in a combination of approval and disbelief. The odd sounds were indeed those of wood being chopped, but the axman who had his back turned to the woods was a flaxen-haired college kid not much taller than the ax itself. No matter how high the boy stood on his toes or how hard he swung, he lacked the size and muscle to handle the heavy ax the way it had been designed to be handled.

But the kid was getting the job done anyway. There was a ragged, gnawed-looking pile of firewood on one side of the chopping stump. On the opposite side was a much bigger, much more intimidating pile of untouched logs.

Rye reined the big black horse closer. He had cut enough wood to know that the boy was overmatched. Game, but in way over his head. He'd be all summer and well into winter before he gnawed his way through that pile of logs.

Then the kid turned around at the sound of Devil's restless snort…and Rye felt as though he had been kicked.

The "boy" was a young woman with the kind of willowy, long-legged, high-breasted body that made a man's blood run hot and thick. What he had thought was a boy's short hair was a mass of platinum braids piled high above a delicate face. Her eyes were a clear amethyst that took away what little breath remained to Rye. She watched him with a combination of curiosity, poise and innocence that reminded him of a Siamese kitten.

Suddenly Rye felt rage replace desire in his blood. *Innocence?* Like flaming hell! She was just one more freeloading female lying in wait for his money—and she had the raw nerve to do it in his favorite retreat.

Rye spurred Devil closer. The girl was not intimidated by the big horse. When Devil's shoulder was no more than a foot away from the girl, Rye reined in and looked her over, trying to reconcile his certainty that she was a cunning gold digger with the slender, delicately beautiful, almost solemn girl who stood watching him with fathomless amethyst eyes, her hand on Devil's shoulder as she absently soothed the restless horse.

Lisa noticed Rye's blunt appraisal for only an instant before she was shaken by a soft, slow explosion deep inside herself, an explosion that sent shock waves all the way to her soul. Emotions sleeted through her, a wild exhilaration mixed with fear, a confused feeling of having lost her footing in reality while at the same time never having felt more alive. And above all she knew a primal certainty that grew with every second she stood motionless watching the stranger who had ridden up and turned her life inside out without saying a word: she had been born to be this man's woman.

There was no hesitation, no withdrawal, no questioning within Lisa as she looked at him. She had lived on the edge of life and death in too many different cultures to flinch from the truth now simply because it was new or strange or utterly unexpected.

She could not look away from him. In electric silence she stared at his dusty boots, his powerful calves and thighs, his narrow hips, his shoulders wide enough to block out the sun, his hard jaw and shadowy beard stubble and curiously sensual mouth—and his eyes the color of rain. She was far too riveted to conceal her fascination with him, and too innocent to understand the currents of sensuality and desire that stirred her body, bringing a slow fever to her flesh.

Rye saw the subtle flush of response in her heightened color and felt a hot shaft of answering desire. Reluctantly he conceded that his father's taste in sexual bait had made a quantum improvement. This candidate was definitely not a thick-hipped, overblown rose. There was an essential elegance to the girl that made him think of the transparent, burning grace of a candle flame. There was also a shimmering, almost hidden sensuality in her that made his body harden in anticipation.

"You're something else, little girl," Rye said finally. "If you'll settle for a diamond bracelet instead of a diamond ring, we'll have a good time for a while."

The words came at Lisa as though from a distance. She blinked and took a deep breath, composing herself in the face of the overwhelming truth of the hard-looking, rough-voiced stranger.

"I beg your pardon?" she asked slowly. "I don't understand."

"The hell you don't," he retorted, ignoring the leap of his blood when he first heard the husky softness of her voice. She was young, almost a girl, but the eyes that watched him were as old—and as curious—as Eve. "I'm a man who doesn't mind paying for what he wants, and you're a girl who doesn't mind getting paid. Just so long as we understand that we'll do fine." His pupils darkened and widened as she took a sudden, sharp breath. "Hell," he added roughly, "we'll do better than fine. We'll burn down the whole damned mountain."

Lisa didn't even hear the last words. Her mind had come to a quivering halt over the description of herself as *a girl who doesn't mind getting paid.* Prostitutes were prostitutes the world over; being described as one by the man who had turned her world inside out just by riding into view made her furious. She realized that he had felt none of the soul-deep awareness that she had felt, had known none of the utter rightness of being with him that she had felt. He had seen only a piece of merchandise he wanted and had set out to purchase it.

The amethyst eyes that examined him were different this time. They noted that his shirt collar and cuffs were badly frayed, a button was missing where the material stretched across his chest, his jeans were faded and worn almost to transparency, and his boots were scarred and down at the heels. This was the wealthy sultan insulting her by offering to rent her body for a while?

Caution vanished in a searing instant, taking with it Lisa's usually excellent self-control. She did something that she hadn't done since she was eight years old. She lost her temper. Completely.

"Who are you trying to fool?" Lisa asked in a voice that had lost all softness. "You couldn't afford a glass stickpin, much less a diamond bracelet."

The look of shock on the man's face made Lisa feel suddenly ashamed of herself for attacking him on the basis of something that she cared nothing about—money. Her shame deepened as she realized that, given the way she had been staring at him, it wasn't surprising that he had assumed she would be pleased rather than angered by his blunt proposition.

Lisa closed her eyes, took a deep breath and remembered something that didn't vary from culture to culture across the world: men, especially poor men, had a great deal of pride, and they were inclined to be quite abrupt when their stomachs were growling.

"If you're hungry, there's bread and bacon," Lisa said in a quiet voice, automatically offering him what food she had. "And cookies," she added, remembering.

The corner of Rye's mouth kicked up in amusement. "Oh, I'm hungry all right," he drawled, "so let's decide on a price."

"But it's free!" Lisa said, shocked that he would expect to pay for a simple meal.

"That's what they all say, and every last one of the poor little dears ends up whining for a diamond ring."

Belatedly Lisa realized that the word *hungry* could have more than one meaning. Her anger flashed again, surprising her. Usually she was the kind of person to laugh rather than swear when things went wrong, but the heat racing through her blood owed nothing to her sense of humor. The man's off-center, lazy, terrifyingly sexy smile made her furious.

"Are you this rude to everyone?" she asked, clipping each word.

"Only to little darlings who ask for it by lying in wait for me in my favorite places."

"I'm here because it's my job. What are you doing in McCall's Meadow besides wasting Boss Mac's time?"

Again, Rye couldn't keep his shock from showing. "Boss Mac?"

"Yes. Boss Mac. The man who pays you to herd cattle. Surely you recognize the name?"

Rye barely swallowed a hoot of incredulous laughter as he realized that the girl had been sent out to trap a man she didn't even know on sight. As he opened his mouth to straighten her out about Boss Mac's true identity, Rye saw the humor of the situation—and the potential for teaching what was obviously an amateur gold digger the rules of the game she had chosen to play.

"I surrender," he murmured, smiling and holding his hands in the air as though she had drawn a gun on him. "I'll be good if you don't report me to, um, Boss Mac." Rye looked down at her and asked innocently, "How well do you know him?"

The change from blunt to charming unsettled Lisa. "I've never met him," she admitted. "I'm just here for the summer, making sure nothing goes wrong with Dr. Thompson's experiment," she added, waving her hand toward the rustic split-rail fence zigzagging across the end of the meadow.

Rye strenuously doubted that she was here only to watch the grass grow, but all he said was, "Well, you watch out for Boss Mac. He's hell on women."

Lisa shrugged gracefully. "He's never bothered me. Neither have his men. All of them have been very polite. With one exception," she added coolly, looking directly at him.

"Sorry about that," Rye said sardonically, lifting his hat in a polite salute. "I'll be real polite from now on. I know Boss Mac well enough to be dead scared of his temper. Is that offer of bacon and bread still open? And cookies."

For a moment Lisa could only stand and look up at Rye's powerful, rangy frame and feel odd sensations shivering throughout her body. The thought of him being hungry, of him needing something that she could give to him, made her feel weak.

"Of course," she said softly, appalled that he would think her so mean as to turn a hungry man away from food. "I'm sorry if I've been rude. My name is Lisa Johansen."

Rye hesitated, unwilling to end the game so

quickly. When he spoke it was curtly, and he gave only the shortened form of his middle name, Ryan. "Rye."

"Rye..." Lisa murmured.

The name intrigued her, as did the man. She wondered if it was his first or his last name or a name he had chosen for himself. She wondered, but she did not ask. She was accustomed to primitive peoples; for them, names were potent magic, often sacred, and always private. She repeated the name again, softly, enjoying it simply because it was his and he had given it to her.

"Rye.... The bacon and bread will be ready in a few minutes. If you want to wash up, there's a pan of water warming in the sun around at the side of the cabin."

Rye's eyes narrowed into glittering silver lines framed by sable lashes that were as thick and as long as a woman's. It was the only hint of softness about him as he studied Lisa, searching for any sign that she was pretending not to know who he really was. He saw absolutely nothing that indicated she knew that he was Edward Ryan McCall III, called Ryan by his dead mother, Rye by his friends, Little Eddy by his father—and Boss Mac by his hired hands.

Rye watched the gentle swinging of Lisa's hips as she walked to the campfire and didn't know whether to be furious or amused that she knew so little about her intended quarry that she didn't even recognize his nickname.

"Little girl, you've got a lot to learn," he muttered under his breath. "And you've come to just the man who can teach you."

3

As Rye watched Lisa's easy, economical movements around the campfire, he decided that his father's latest candidate was different in more than her unusual, delicate beauty. Whatever else Rye might think about her, she wasn't afraid of work. Not only had she been willing to tackle a log with an ax that was old, dull and far too big for her, she had also taken the time to clear up the clutter that had slowly gathered around the cabin over the summers of student use. Used aluminum cans, plastic containers and glass bottles, as well as other flotsam and jetsam of modern life, were all stacked in neat piles at the side of the cabin.

"Next time I come, I'll bring a gunnysack and pack out that trash for you," he offered.

Lisa looked up from the frying bacon. The pan was perched on a warped, blackened grate, which was supported by the rocks that she had brought from the stream to make a fire ring. "Trash?"

"The bottles and cans," he said, gesturing toward the side of the cabin.

"Oh."

Lisa frowned slightly as she turned the bacon. Where she had come from, the pile would have been viewed as raw materials rather than junk. Broken glass would have been patiently ground into jewelry or pressure-flaked until it was a knife edge that could cut tough fibers or hides. It was a technique that she had used more than once herself, when they had lived with tribes that were too poor or too remotely located to replace steel knives when they broke or were lost. Modern steel kept its edge miraculously, but it was an expensive miracle. As for the tough, resilient plastic bottles, they would have been used to carry water, seeds, flour or salt—or even, on the shores of an African lake, as floats for fishing nets. The aluminum cans would have been worried over until they became something useful or were reluctantly discarded somewhere along the way.

"Thank you," Lisa said carefully. "If it's all right, I'd like to hang on to some of those things for now. The gunnysack would be very nice, though, if you're through with it. That way I can soak clothes in the stream and not lose them. The water runs awfully fast."

Rye stared, unable to believe that he had heard correctly about the collection of junk along the side of the cabin and washing clothes in the stream. Even if he put the question of trash aside, the other student caretakers had gone into town once a week for supplies and laundry and had carried enough equipment up the trail in the first place to make two of his best packhorses groan.

With the exception of the frying pan and bucket, it didn't look as though Lisa had carried anything new to the cabin. Her clothes were clean but showed signs of long wearing. There were patches on her jeans and shirt that had been sewn on with incredibly tiny, even stitches. He had assumed that the patches and fading were part of the new fashion trend that had clothes looking old the first time they were worn out of the shop. Now he was beginning to wonder. Maybe it was simply that she preferred to wear old, comfortable clothing as he did.

Or maybe she just didn't have a choice.

Lisa didn't notice Rye's suddenly speculative look at her clothes. She was busy cutting another piece of bacon from the slab that Lassiter had brought. She was using a broken jackknife she had discovered among the weeds in the front yard. Unfortunately she hadn't discovered a whetstone with the knife. She had ground off the rust on a convenient rock, but the blade would have had a tough time gnawing through butter.

With a muttered word in another language, Lisa set aside the hopelessly dull knife and went to the side of the cabin. She selected a piece of glass, examined its edge and returned to the fire. Casually she went back to work on the bacon, holding the glass between thumb and forefinger and cutting with light, quick strokes. When she was finished, she set the impromptu blade aside on top of a flat rock that she had found and carried to the fire for just that purpose.

"Hell of a knife," Rye said, not bothering to conceal his amazement.

"It won't hold its edge for long," Lisa said, laying the strip of bacon in the cast-iron pan, "but while it does, it's sharper than any steel."

"Lose your knife?" he asked, approaching the topic from another angle.

"No. It's just that the one I found was pretty rusty. Must have been here for a long time."

"Umm. I'll be going into town tomorrow. Want me to pick up a new knife for you?"

Lisa glanced up and smiled at Rye, silently thanking him for his thoughtfulness. "That's very nice of you, but I found enough glass around here to last for several summers."

She turned back to the bacon, missing the look that crossed Rye's face.

"Glass," he said neutrally.

She nodded. "And there are enough antlers around to keep an edge on."

"Enough antlers."

Something in Rye's tone caught Lisa's attention. She looked up, saw his face and laughed softly, realizing how she must have sounded.

"You use a point of the antler to pressure-flake the glass when the edge goes dull," she explained. "Glass has a conchoidal fracture. It breaks in tiny curves rather than a straight line. So you just put the point of the antler on the edge of the glass, press, and a tiny curved flake comes off. You do that all the way down the edge and then up the other side if you want to be fancy. The blade you get is pretty uneven, but it's hellishly sharp. For a while."

There was a silence while Rye assimilated what had been said and tried to match it with Lisa's deceptively fragile beauty.

"Are you one of those crazy physical anthropology students who run around trying to live like Stone Age men?" he demanded finally.

Lisa's soft laughter and amused amethyst eyes made tiny tongues of fire lick over Rye's nerve endings.

"Close," she admitted, still smiling. "My parents are anthropologists who study the daily life of the most primitive cultures on earth. Hunter-gatherers, nomads—you name it and we've lived it. Mom got interested in rare grasses, so she started collecting seeds and plants wherever we were and sending them on to university seed banks. The people who were working to develop high-yield, disease-resistant crops for Third World countries would use the plants in their experiments. That's why I'm here."

"You're disease resistant and high yield?" Rye offered dryly. He was rewarded by musical feminine laughter that shortened his breath.

"No, I'm an experienced seed collector who is used to camping out."

"In a word, just right for a summer stint in McCall's Meadow."

She nodded as she looked around at the clean, fertile meadow and the aspens shivering against a bottomless blue sky. "Of all the places I've been, this is the most beautiful," she said softly, closing her eyes for an instant to drink the sensual pleasures of the meadow. She inhaled softly, her lips slightly parted as she tasted the untamed wind. "Sweet, pure, perfect," she murmured. "Do you have any idea how very rare something like this is?"

Rye looked at Lisa's sensual appreciation of the sun and sky and wind for a long moment. The certainty grew in him that he had been wrong about her. She was what she had called the meadow—sweet, pure, perfect and very, very rare. She wasn't just another woman lined up for a lifetime of easy living as a rich man's wife. She couldn't be. Every one of the women who had come hunting him at the ranch had been appalled by the lack of amenities in the ranch house—the bare wood floors and stainless steel silverware, the ancient kitchen—and by his blunt promise that any work that got done around the house would be done by his wife rather than a pack of servants. And that went for the stables, as well. Any woman who wanted to ride could damn well shovel out stalls, polish saddles and bridles, and in general earn the right to put a horse through its paces.

Every single one of the women had told Rye to go to hell and had left without a backward look—which was exactly what he had had in mind. He didn't think Lisa would do that. She didn't have fancy nails to worry about. Hers were short enough not to get in the way, and they were as scrupulously clean as the wisps of platinum-blond hair that clung to her delicately flushed face. Nor did the thought of physical labor dismay her. He could still see her in his mind's eye, stretching up on tiptoe in a futile effort to bring the ax blade down with enough force to take a decent bite out of the log. She had spent a long time working on that log, long enough to leave red marks on the palms of her small hands.

He could see those marks clearly as she piled steaming, herb-scented bread and evenly cooked, crisp bacon on a plate for him.

"After dinner, I'll chop some wood for you," Rye said, his tone gruff. The thought of Lisa struggling to chop enough wood simply to cook his food disturbed Rye in ways that he didn't understand.

Lisa's hands paused as she put bacon on the battered tin plate. She didn't want Rye to feel that he had to repay her for the food he was eating. The longer she looked at his clothes, the more she doubted that he could afford even the most token amount of cash in payment. Nor did she want it. At the same time, she knew how proud a poor man could be.

"Thank you," she said softly. "I'm not very good with an ax. The places where we've lived didn't have pieces of wood big enough to need chopping before they were burned in cooking fires."

Rye bit into the camp bread and closed his eyes in pure pleasure. Tender, fragrant, steamy, exotic, the bread was like nothing he had ever eaten before. Food always tasted better in the meadow's crisp, high-mountain air, but this was extraordinary.

"Best bread I've ever eaten," he said simply. "What did you put in it?"

"There's a kind of wild onion growing near the stream," Lisa said as she settled cross-legged on the ground. "There was something that smelled remarkably like sage, too, and another plant that was very like parsley. I could see that deer had been browsing on the plants, so I knew they weren't poisonous. They tasted good when I nibbled on them. Kind of clean and crisp and lively. I put a little of each in for flavoring. Bread may be the staff of life, but variety is the spice."

Rye's grin flashed suddenly, making a hard white curve against his tanned face. Then he frowned as he thought over what she had said about tasting the various meadow greenery. "Maybe you better take it easy on the plants."

Her head snapped up. "I didn't go into the fenced part of the meadow."

"That's not what I meant. Some of those plants might make you sick."

"Then deer wouldn't eat them," Lisa said reasonably. "Don't worry. Before I came up here, I spent some time in the university library. I know exactly what the local narcotic and psychoactive plants look like."

"Psychoactive? *Narcotic?*"

"Ummm," she agreed, swallowing a bite of bacon. "Hallucinations and delirium or narcosis and full respiratory arrest, that sort of thing."

"From my meadow plants?" he asked incredulously.

Lisa smiled over Rye's proprietary "my" in reference to the meadow. She knew just how he felt. After only two weeks in the meadow, she felt as though it were her home.

"There's a plant growing not thirty feet from here that can cure the symptoms of asthma, make you crazy or kill you, depending on the dose," she said matter-of-factly. "It's called datura. Grows everywhere in the world. I recognized it right away."

Rye looked suddenly at the bread he had been wolfing down.

"Don't worry," Lisa said quickly. "I wouldn't touch datura. It's simply too powerful. The only herbs I use are for flavoring or for simple things like a headache or a stomachache or to soak my hands to help them to heal faster after hard work."

"There are things for that around here?" Rye asked, looking at the meadow and forest with new interest.

Lisa nodded because her mouth was too full to talk politely. Other cultures didn't object to a person chewing and talking at the same time, but Americans did. Her parents had been quite emphatic on that point. Burping was also prohibited. On the plus side, however, it was not considered a sign of demonic possession in this culture to eat with the left hand. That was quite a relief to Lisa, because she was naturally left-handed.

"Almost all modern drugs are the result of research into what is called 'folk medicine,'" Lisa continued. "Outside of the industrialized nations, people still depend on herbalists and home remedies to heal the sick. For ordinary discomfort such things work quite well and, compared to Western medicines, they cost almost nothing. Of course, when they get the chance, every tribe, no matter how primitive, inoculates their children against contagious diseases, and families will travel hundreds of miles at terrible hardship to take a sick or badly injured child to a hospital."

Rye savored the subtly flavored bread as he asked questions and listened to Lisa talking matter-of-factly about exotic cultures and various tribes' special expertise in medicine or animal husbandry or astronomy. Before he had finished eating, he had begun to wonder about his definition of "primitive." Lisa had been raised among tribes that could be described in no other terms than savage, primitive, Stone Age, yet there was a sophistication about her that had nothing to do with fine clothes, finishing schools or the other hallmarks of modern civilization. Lisa accepted human diversity with tolerance, humor, appreciation and intelligence. She was the most cosmopolitan and at the same time the most innocent person he had ever met.

The longer Rye sat with Lisa, the more convinced he became that the patches on her clothes weren't a fashion flourish but a necessity. Nor was the fact that she gathered trash for future use an attempt to be eccentric or ecologically trendy; she did indeed have a specific use for what she kept. She sat with lithe grace on the ground not because she had taken yoga or ballet, but because she had been raised among cultures that had no chairs.

"Amazing," he muttered to himself.

"I suppose so," Lisa said, grimacing. "I never went in for fermented mare's milk myself. The smell is indescribable. I guess that by the time we moved in with the Bedouins, I was just too old to be flexible in my tastes."

Rye realized that she had overheard him and thought that he was commenting on the Bedouin passion for fermented mare's milk rather than on his own awareness of how different Lisa was from other women he had met.

"I'll stick to bourbon," Rye said, trying and mercifully failing to imagine what fermented mare's milk would taste like.

"I'll stick to mountain air," Lisa said. "And mountain water."

The tone of her voice told Rye that she meant it. Having been raised in a dry, hot part of Texas, he could understand her passion for altitude and cold, sweet water.

"Time to earn my meal," he said, coming to his feet.

"You don't have to."

"How about if I admit that I like chopping wood?"

"How about if I admit that I don't believe you?" she retorted, looking at her own reddened palms.

He grinned. "I'm a lot tougher than you are. Besides, there's something satisfying about cutting wood. You can see exactly what you've done. Beats hell out of pushing papers and sitting on twelve corporate boards."

"I'll have to take your word for it," she said, glancing up at him curiously.

Abruptly Rye realized that a down-at-the-heels cowboy wouldn't know anything about corporate boards. He ducked his head and examined the ax blade carefully, cursing his heedless tongue. He was almost sure that Lisa didn't have the slightest idea who he was—either that, or she was a world-class actress. Somehow he doubted that she was. He did know one thing: innocent or actress, he didn't want her to realize that he was rich. He didn't want the flashes of elemental feminine appreciation that he had seen in her eyes when she looked at him turn into an equally elemental fem-

inine calculation as she added up her own poverty
and his real net worth.

"Both blades look like they've been used to
quarry stone," Rye muttered.

He went to where he had tied Devil and fished
around in the saddlebags he always carried. A few
moments later he came back to the campfire with
a whetstone in his hand and went to work sharp-
ening the ax. Lisa watched, admiring his unusually
long, strong fingers and the skill with which he
worked to bring an edge up on the steel.

Once Rye glanced up and saw Lisa looking in-
tently at his hands. He thought of what it would
be like to be touching her silky body instead of
cold steel, and to have her watching him. Immediately the fever that had been prowling in his
blood became hotter, heavier, like his heartbeat.
He bent over and went back to work on the ax,
not wanting the direction of his thoughts to be revealed by his hardening body.

"Better," he grunted finally, touching his fingertip to the edge, "but it needs a lot of work
before I'd want to shave with it."

Rye stepped up to one of the logs that Lassiter
had dragged into camp, swung the ax and felt the
blade sink into the wood. He had learned a lot
about chopping wood the summer he made the
split-rail fence that kept cattle from grazing in
McCall's Meadow. Barbwire would have been

easier to install but he had preferred to look at weathered wood zigzagging over the remote, beautiful meadow.

When Lisa finished cleaning up, she found a spot that was covered with pine needles and warmed by the fading sun. She sat and watched Rye, fascinated by his combination of power and masculine grace. The sound of the ax biting into wood was clean, sharp, rhythmic. It went on without pause or change until he bent to reposition the log. Then the rhythm resumed as muscles bunched across his shoulders, straining the fabric of the old shirt. The pile of cut wood grew with astonishing speed as the late-afternoon silence was punctuated by the whistling strike of steel against wood and the small sounds of chips falling to the ground amid dry aspen leaves.

Suddenly Rye's shirt split as the worn fabric gave up the unequal contest against the shifting power of his shoulder muscles.

Lisa leaped to her feet and ran toward him. "Your shirt!" she said, dismayed.

The back of Rye's shirt had parted in a wide, straight tear. Between the pieces of faded blue cloth, his skin gleamed over the flex and play of his muscles as he continued chopping wood without pausing to assess the damage to his clothes. Lisa's breath wedged in her throat and stayed there. The satin heat of him was tangible, as was the raw strength that had torn apart the cloth. Watching him sent the most curious sensations through her body, a shimmering feeling that made her skin flush as though with fever.

"No problem," Rye said, glancing at Lisa as he lifted the ax again.

"But you wouldn't have ruined your shirt if you hadn't been chopping wood for me," she said, biting her lip.

"Sure I would have." Rye paused to balance a chunk of log on the chopping stump. He raised the ax and brought it down on the wood with a smooth, uninterrupted motion. The wood split apart and the halves tumbled to the ground. "The shirt's nearly as old as I am. I should have tossed it out long ago. I just kind of liked it."

"Toss it? Do you mean throw it away?"

He smiled. She made it sound as though throwing away the worn shirt was unthinkable.

"Oh, no, don't," Lisa said, shaking her head in a quick negative. "Leave it with me. I'll mend it."

"You'll mend it?" he asked in disbelief, looking at the frayed cuffs. The shirt wasn't worth the thread that it would take to fix it, much less the time.

"Of course," she said. "There's no need for you to buy a new shirt to replace this one. Really."

Rye sank the ax blade into the chopping stump and turned toward Lisa. She looked as unhappy as her voice had been when she had told him that it was her fault that his shirt was ruined.

"Please," she said softly, putting her hand on his arm.

"It's all right, honey," he said, touching her cheek with gentle, callused fingertips. "I don't blame you."

Lisa couldn't control the quiver of awareness that swept through her at Rye's touch. When he saw the telltale trembling of her flesh, heat flooded violently through him. He looked from her fingers tightening on his arm to her suddenly dilated pupils and knew that she wanted him. She believed that he was too poor to replace a worn-out shirt, yet she shivered helplessly when he touched her.

The realization swept through Rye, and with it came the knowledge that he had never wanted a woman half so much as he wanted the one who stood only inches away, watching him with wide amethyst eyes as she tried to still the trembling of her lower lip by catching it between her small teeth.

"Lisa..." he whispered, but there were no words to tell her about the fever raging just beneath the surface of his control.

He fitted his hard hand beneath her chin and bent down to her. It took an agonizing amount of willpower to do no more than barely brush his lips over hers, soothing their trembling. She stiffened at the touch and then shivered wildly once again.

Rye forced himself to release Lisa when all he wanted to do was to undress her, to pour over her like a hot, heavy rain, to feel her pouring over him in turn....

Then he looked at her eyes. They were wide with surprise and curiosity and perhaps desire. He didn't know. She hadn't responded to his kiss by offering more of her mouth to him or by putting her arms around him. Perhaps she sensed the desire running through him in a savage flood and was afraid of him. She was barely more than a girl, and she was alone in a remote place with a man who was easily twice her strength—a man who wanted her with a violence that he could barely control.

The realization of his own savage need and Lisa's helplessness shocked Rye.

"It's all right, little one," he said huskily. "I won't hurt you."

4

The memory of Lisa's trusting, almost shy smile stayed with Rye all the way down the mountain. So did the heat in his blood. He had intended to teach her how to use the ax. He hadn't dared. He hadn't trusted himself to stand that close to her. He had ached to take more from Lisa than that single, brushing kiss, yet he hadn't allowed himself even to touch the tip of his tongue to her soft lips. Smelling the sunshine scent of her hair, seeing the tiny trembling of her lips, breathing in the sweetness of her breath... It had been all he could do to keep from unwrapping her shining braids and pulling her unbound hair around him, binding them together in a world that began and ended with their joined bodies.

With a throttled groan, Rye turned his thoughts away from the shimmering temptation of Lisa Johansen. It didn't seem possible that any girl in that day and age could be so innocent, yet she had acted as though she had never been kissed. Certainly she hadn't seemed to know how to return even that chaste caress with a gliding pressure of her own lips.

The thought of such complete innocence shocked, intrigued and aroused Rye. The women he had known before had been experienced, sophisticated, sure of what they wanted from him. Sometimes he had taken what they so willingly offered. Most of the time he simply had walked away, disgusted by seeing dollar signs reflected in the women's eyes rather than real desire.

More than Lisa's delicate beauty and her unusual upbringing, it was her honest sensuality that made her so compelling to Rye. She didn't know that he was rich. She didn't look at him and see more money than a reasonable person could spend in a lifetime. She looked at him and saw a man.

And she wanted the man she saw.

Rye had sensed Lisa's passionate fascination with him as surely as he had sensed her inexperience. The fact that he himself—rather than his bank account and future inheritance—aroused Lisa was so unexpected that Rye could barely allow himself to believe it. The fact that his touch made her shiver with sensual fever rather than with greedy fantasies of money everlasting was so compelling that Rye hadn't been able to trust himself to remain with Lisa in the meadow's sun-drenched intimacy.

By the time he reached the ranch house, he had decided that he must have an objective way to judge Lisa's apparent innocence and honesty. It was as obvious as the fit of his jeans that he wanted her too much to trust his own judgment of her character. He very much wanted to believe that she was exactly what she seemed, completely un-awakened yet feeling the slow heat of desire spreading through her innocence whenever she looked up at him.

Rye pulled off his torn shirt and wadded it up for the wastebasket. Just before he let go of the cloth, he hesitated. He had finally promised Lisa that he would let her try to mend the shirt. She had been so relieved that he had almost told her that he could buy all the shirts he wanted, anytime he wanted them. Then the thought of her slender hands working over the shirt, touching each fold and seam, leaving something of herself in the cloth and then giving it back to him had changed his mind. He would far, far rather have her believe that he was too poor to buy himself a shirt than to have her know that he was rich and getting richer with every day.

Ignoring the ranch account books that lay wait-ing within the floppy disk, Rye bypassed the com-puter for the telephone. He dialed a number, waited and heard Dr. Thompson answer on the fourth ring.

"Ted? This is Rye McCall. I want to talk to you about that student you sent up to watch the meadow this summer."

"You mean Lisa Johansen? She's not a student, at least not officially. She challenged our anthropology department. As soon as the tests are graded, I'm willing to bet she'll be a graduate, not a student. Of course, with her parents, it's not surprising. The Drs. Johansen are world-famous experts on—"

"Challenged?" interrupted Rye quickly, knowing that if he didn't get Dr. Thompson off the subject of anthropology, it could be a long time before they got back to the subject of Lisa Johansen. The professor was a wonderful teacher and a good friend, but he could talk a mountain flat.

"Challenged. As in took final exams in certain courses without having taken the courses themselves," Dr. Thompson said. "When you have someone with Lisa's unconventional educational background, it's the only way to test academic achievement. The poor girl's never been in a real classroom, you know."

Rye hadn't known, but beyond making appropriate encouraging noises, he said nothing. He had Dr. Thompson steered in the right direction. Now all Rye had to do was settle into a comfortable chair and let nature take its inevitable course.

"Oh, yes, it's true," Dr. Thompson continued. "She speaks several exotic languages, she can transform unspeakable things into savory stews over a campfire, and she can do clever things with her hands that make some of my physical anthropology students' eyes pop. Wait until you see her make a deadly little knife out of a piece of broken beer bottle."

Rye's gentle murmur of encouragement was lost in the professor's rushing words.

"She's a darling child, too. Such eyes. My Lord, I haven't seen eyes like that since her mother was my first and best student years and years ago. Lisa's a lot like her mother. Fine mind, healthy body, and not enough money to make a call from a pay phone—not that she would know how to, either. Lisa, that is, not her mother. Poor child barely knew how to flush a toilet when she got here. As for a modern kitchen, forget it. My electric stove frustrated her, the dishwasher made her jump and the trash compactor completely boggled her. Rather unnerved me, if you want to know the truth. Now I know how the natives feel when my eager students follow them around taking notes on odd indigenous customs. She learns fast, though. A very bright girl. Very bright indeed. Still, her parents waited too long to send her here. Now all she's suited for is the life of a vagabond herder.''

"Why?"

"Time. Yesterday, today, tomorrow."

"I don't understand."

The professor sighed. "Neither does Lisa. Civilized man divided time into past, present and future. Many tribes don't. To them, there are only two kinds of time. There is a very vague 'time before' and then there is the vast, undifferentiated *now*. That's where Lisa lives. In the endless tribal present. She no more understands the Western concepts of hourly work and weekly wages than I understand Zulu. As for typewriters, filing cabinets, computers and that sort of thing…well, there's just no possibility. The only suitable job I could find for her on short notice was watching grass grow in your meadow until the school year begins in the fall. Then her scholarship money should take care of her until Geoffrey gets back from Alice after Christmas.''

"Geoffrey? Alice?" asked Rye, wondering how the conversation had been sidetracked.

"Geoffrey is the brightest anthropology student I've had since Lisa's mother. Alice Springs is in Australia's outback. Geoffrey is doing research for his Ph.D. on the oral traditions of Australian aborigines, with particular emphasis on the use of—''

"Does Lisa know this Geoffrey?" Rye interrupted impatiently, feeling an irrational shaft of jealousy.

"Not yet, but she will. She's going to marry him."

"What?"

"Lisa's going to marry Geoffrey. Haven't you been listening? Lisa's parents sent her to me so that I could find a suitable husband for her. I have. Geoffrey Langdon. Her skills are admirably matched with his professional needs. She'll be able to run the camp while he works. Who knows? If she shows the same flair her mother did for fieldwork, Lisa might be able to help Geoffrey on his research."

"What does Geoffrey think of all this?"

"I haven't got an answer from him yet, but I can't imagine that he would be anything except enthusiastic. She's a pretty little thing and her parents are very, very well respected within academic circles. That sort of thing matters to young academics, you know. He might even get to work with her parents, perhaps even to collaborate with them on a paper or two. That would be a colossal boost for his academic career."

"What would Lisa get out of this love feast?" Rye asked, trying to keep the irritation from his voice.

"'Love feast?' Oh, dear, you *are* a child of

Western culture, aren't you? Love has nothing to do with it. Lisa will get out of the arrangement exactly what women have always gotten out of marriage—a lifetime of food, shelter and protection. In Lisa's case, that's much more necessary than love. She simply isn't prepared to cope with the modern Western world. That's why her parents sent her to me when it came time for her to marry."

"She came here to find a husband?" Rye asked harshly.

"Of course. She could hardly marry a Bedouin herder, could she?"

There was a silence, which was immediately filled by Dr. Thompson's blithe retelling of the life of a Bedouin wife. Rye barely listened. He was still caught in the moment when his worst fears had been confirmed: Lisa was one more woman looking for a lifetime meal ticket. Innocence had nothing to do with it. The game was as old as Adam and Eve—male lust and female calculation joined in unholy matrimony.

And Rye had nearly fallen right into the musk-scented tiger trap.

Afterward Rye couldn't remember the rest of the conversation. He showered and changed clothes in a bleak rage, not knowing whether he was more angry with Lisa for being so innocently, deliciously treacherous or with himself for almost falling into her hands as though he had no more brains than a ripe apple.

Yet no matter how he swore at himself or at her, the memory of Lisa's trembling mouth haunted him, and when he fell asleep it was to dream of velvet heat enfolding him, caressing him, arousing him until he awakened with a stifled cry on his lips. His body was sweating, hard, heavy with a desire so great it was almost unbearable.

It was no better the following morning. Rye stepped into the bathroom cursing. After fifteen minutes he decided that cold showers were vastly overrated as a means of subduing lust. He stamped into his boots and ate a cold breakfast, because he knew that the smell of bread toasting would have brought back memories of camp bread and Lisa watching him, her fingers trembling almost invisibly as she handed him the fragrant, steaming food she had prepared for him.

Rye slammed the kitchen door and strode out to the barn, wishing that he could slam the door on his thoughts half so easily. In the east, rugged peaks were condensing out of the dawn sky. The cowhands were straggling out to the barn. Horses nickered and milled in the corral, waiting for men to single them out with flying lariats and gentle words.

"Morning, Boss Mac. Old Devil looks like he

got some of the starch taken out of him yesterday.''

Rye recognized the pale silver of Lassiter's hair even before the cowhand's drawl registered. ''Morning, Lassiter. I took Devil up the back way to the meadow. You look a little tuckered around the edges yourself. Tough ride?''

The cowhand grinned, lifted his hat to smooth his prematurely silver hair and seated his hat once more with a swift stroke. ''I was meaning to thank you. Cherry said you particularly told her to look me up for a ride. That filly was prime, really prime.''

''Bet she came with a meat inspector's stamp on her haunch to prove it, too,'' Rye said sardonically.

Lassiter shook his head. ''Boss, you shouldn't take it so personal. When a gal that looks like that is ready, willing and by God *able*, why the least a man can do is meet her halfway.''

''That's why I have you around. Fastest zipper in the West.''

The retort and the cowhand's hoot of laughter drew smiles from the men who were hauling saddles out to the corral fence. Lassiter's ability to get women into bed was legend. No one knew whether it was his silver hair, his slow smile or his quick hands. Whatever it was, the women loved it.

"How did the meadow look?" Lassiter asked innocently.

"Better than my dining room."

"Yeah, Cherry mentioned something about that. Was she really checking the silver?"

"She sure as hell was. Did she take the fillings out of your teeth?"

"It was worth every last one. Did you eat supper there?"

"In the dining room?"

Lassiter's eyes twinkled. "In the meadow."

Rye grunted, then gave in. Lassiter would keep waltzing around the subject of Lisa until he found out how Rye had reacted to having his private domain invaded by yet another woman. If there was anything on earth the cowhands loved better than a joke, Rye hadn't found out what it might be.

"At least she can cook," Rye said obliquely.

"Easy on the eyes, too. Skinny, though, 'cept up top."

Rye started to deny that Lisa was skinny anywhere, then caught the gleam in Lassiter's eyes. Rye laughed and shook his head.

"I should brand your tail for not warning me about Cherry or Lisa," Rye said.

Lassiter's teeth flashed. "You find a filly that can rope and hog-tie me, and you can put that brand anywhere you please."

"I think I already found one."

"Yeah?"

"Yeah. You've been up to the meadow so often your bay's big hooves left a trench."

Slowly Lassiter shook his head. "Not that filly. Miss Lisa's too innocent for the likes of me."

"Besides," Jim called from the corral, "she ain't given him nothing but the same sweet smile she gives every other hand. And bread and bacon that would make a stone weep. Lordy, that gal can make campfire food sit up and do tricks."

Rye was relieved to hear that Lisa hadn't responded to any of the cowhands as she had to him. However, that did nothing to cool his anger at himself for almost being taken in by her.

"Innocent? Maybe, but she's after the same thing Cherry was—a diamond ring and a free ride for life. Only difference is that Lisa doesn't know who I am."

"Didn't you introduce yourself?" Lassiter asked, surprised.

"Sure. As just plain Rye."

Instantly Lassiter saw the humorous possibilities in the situation. He smiled slowly, then laughed and laughed. Reluctantly Rye smiled.

"She thinks you're just another hand?" Jim asked, looking from Lassiter to Rye.

"Yeah," Rye said.

Jim chuckled. "An' she's looking for a husband?"

"Yeah."

"An' she don't know who you really are?"

"Yeah."

"I don't believe it. She's no hip-swinging city hussy."

"Ask Dr. Thompson the next time he comes up to the meadow," Rye said in clipped tones.

"Well, shoot," Jim complained. "She sure didn't let any of us in on the game. Don't blame her for passing up old Lassiter as hitching material, but she didn't give Blaine a second look, neither. Ain't that so, Blaine?"

"That's right," called a tall, lean young man who was squatting on his heels in front of the corral, smoking a cigarette. "An' the good Lord knows I'm a durn sight prettier than Lassiter."

There were catcalls and howls from the cowhands as they compared Blaine's prowess and physical attributes to Lassiter's. Both men took the chaffing with good nature. They had played too many jokes on the other cowhands to object when their own turn came to be the butt of rough humor. Rye waited until there was a pause in the raillery before he got down to implementing the decision that he had made in the small hours of the night when he had awakened sweating with desire.

"Well, I'm tired of being chased and cornered on my own land," Rye said flatly.

There were murmurs of agreement on the part

of the hands. A man's ranch was his castle—or
ought to be. Boss Mac had their sympathy in his
struggle against matrimony.

"Lisa doesn't know who I am and I want it to
stay that way. As long as she thinks I'm just one
of the hands she'll treat me like one of you. That's
what I want. Otherwise I won't be able to spend
any time in the meadow at all without being pes-
tered to death."

There was another round of agreement from the
men. Each of them knew how much Boss Mac
loved to spend time in his meadow. They also
knew that without the meadow to soothe him, Boss
Mac had a temper that would back down a hungry
bear.

"Now, I know one of you would call me Boss
Mac if I went up to the meadow with you, so I
won't. When I go, I'll go alone. Got that?"

There were grins all around as the men thought
about the dimensions of the unfolding joke. There
was Lisa up in the meadow hunting a marriageable
man, and the most hunted, marriageable man in
five states would be slipping in and out of the
meadow without her even suspecting it.

"And I want you to stop going up there."

The grins vanished. A joke was one thing. Leaving a small bit of a girl out in the wilderness completely on her own was another. No matter how
well she cooked over a fire, and no matter how

game she was in taking on a man's tasks, she was
neither as big nor as strong as a man. In the West,
such distinctions still brought out latent stirrings
of chivalry. The cowhands would tease Lisa un-
mercifully, play a thousand jokes on her without
a second thought, but they would never do anything that they believed would actually harm her.

As one, the men looked to Lassiter, who was
their unofficial spokesman as well as the Rocking
M's foreman.

"You sure that's wise, boss?" Lassiter asked
softly. "That there meadow is a long ways away
from anywhere. What if she turned her ankle on a
wet rock or the ax slipped when she was chopping
wood or the summer flu got her and she was too
weak to carry a bucket of water from the stream?"

Only the rosy flush of dawn kept Rye's face
from showing a sudden pallor. The idea of Lisa
being hurt, alone and stranded up in the high
meadow camp was unthinkable. She had been so
at home around the camp, so supremely suited to
her surroundings, that he had forgotten the true
primitiveness of the meadow.

"You're right," Rye said instantly. "I should
have thought of that. Go up, but not as often as
you've been going, or else no work will get done
and I'll never have the meadow to myself." He
looked slowly from man to man, including everyone in the cool glance. "But if any man touches

her, he'll be looking for a new arm and a new job, in that order. Understood?''

Male smiles flashed briefly in the dawn. They understood very well, and they approved.

"Sure thing, boss," Lassiter said. "And thanks for the visiting privileges. She makes the best bread I ever ate. Think maybe she'd like to be a ranch cook after she's through watching grass grow this summer?''

"Doubt it. By then she'll have given up on Edward McCall III and moved on to greener pastures.''

Rye stood in the flooding rush of dawn and wondered why the thought of Lisa leaving brought restlessness rather than relief.

5

Polaroid camera in hand, Lisa slipped through the split-rail fence into the meadow preserve. She went to the nearest numbered stake—number five—knelt and looked through the viewfinder. The silvery-green grass in front of the stake was slender and delicate, almost fragile appearing, but it had grown inches in the past week.

"Good for you, number five," she muttered. "Keep it up and you'll go to the head of Dr. Thompson's list of hardy, useful grasses. Your children will be fruitful and multiply in pastures all over the world."

She let out her breath, squeezed the button and heard the surprisingly loud clack and grind of the Polaroid's mechanism as the camera went to work. Instantly a featureless square popped out of the bottom of the camera box. She shielded the print from the sun by putting it in her shirt pocket where the exotic chemicals could develop in peace. After weeks in the meadow, the process of development was no longer so fascinating that she watched each print as it condensed out of nothing until it filled the odd paper square. These days she contented herself with sneaking quick peeks as the photo developed. She couldn't quite take the process for granted. There were too many parts of the world where the camera and its instant images would have been considered magic, and she had lived in most of them.

The tribal view of photographs as magic was one that Lisa came close to sharing. Even after Dr. Thompson had given her a book on the photochemical process, she still felt like a magician with a very special kind of magic wand every time she wielded the Polaroid and came up with precise, hand-sized images of the world around her. It was certainly easier than the painstaking process of exactly reproducing the appearance of all the plants with paper and pencil, as her mother did.

Lisa went through the meadow, photographing the plants in front of each numbered stake, changing packs of film several times. If Boss Mac's cowhands hadn't delivered fresh film, she would have been forced to go "down the hill" and into town every week. She preferred staying in the meadow, where time had nothing to do with clocks.

Seasons she understood. There was a time of fertility and a time of growth, a time of harvest and a time of barren fields. That was predictable and natural, like the rising and setting of the sun or the waxing and waning of the moon. It was just the artificial nature of weeks that took some getting used to. She suspected that for the rest of her life she would think of a week as the time it took to use up five packs of Polaroid film in McCall's Meadow.

As Lisa worked she kept pausing to stand on tiptoe and peer toward the grove of mixed aspen and evergreens at the back of the cabin. Rye would come up that way, when he came. If he came. Since the first time he had visited the meadow, he had returned twice a week and had hardly spoken to her at all. Once she had followed the tracks of his horse to the sheer trail zigzagging down the shoulder of the mountain. None of Boss Mac's other cowhands had come into the meadow by that route. Nor were there other tracks on the trail besides those of Rye's big black horse. Apparently it was a trail only Rye knew about—or dared to take.

Would he come today?

The thought brought a surge of the same restlessness that had claimed Lisa's dreams since the first time she had met Rye. She had enjoyed the visits of Boss Mac's men, but Rye's visits the past few weeks had been different. His effect on her was too vivid, too overwhelming, to be described by a word as bland as "enjoyment." He was a summer storm sweeping down from the peaks, leaving everything in his path wind-tossed and shivery and glistening with new possibilities.

She could relive in her memory the single time he had kissed her weeks before, the slow brush of his lips over her mouth, the warmth of his breath, the heat radiating from his big body into hers. When he had kissed her, she had been too shocked by the sensations bursting through her to do more than stand motionless, consumed by the instant when she had first known a man's kiss. By the time she had truly realized what was happening, he was already stepping away from her. He had gone back to chopping wood as though nothing had happened, leaving her to wonder whether he had been half so shaken by the caress as she had been.

"Of course he wasn't," Lisa muttered as she switched a used film pack for a fresh one and aimed the viewfinder at another numbered stake. "If he had been, he would have kissed me again. Besides, kissing isn't unusual here. Look at the kids who were in Dr. Thompson's eight o'clock class. Half of them were late to class because they were kissing their lovers goodbye in the corridor.

The rest of them brought their lovers right into class and—oh, darn it, I ruined another one!''

Glumly Lisa stuck the botched photo in her rear pocket without waiting to see how badly out of focus the print was. She had to stop thinking about Rye and kissing and lovers. It made her whole body tremble. That was the third photo she had mangled so far today. At that rate she would need an extra shipment of film before the week was out.

Maybe Rye would bring it.

With a groan of exasperation at her own unruly mind, Lisa went to the next stake—and saw Rye walking across the meadow toward her. She knew him instantly, even though he was too far away to make out his features. No other man moved with just that blend of male grace and power, his long-legged stride eating up the distance between them. No other man had shoulders like that, a breadth and strength balanced above lean hips. And, Lisa thought as Rye drew closer, no man had ever watched her the way he did, with a combination of curiosity and hunger in his eyes. And wariness.

The wariness had been there the second time Rye had visited Lisa in the meadow, and it hadn't changed since then. She had noticed his attitude immediately and had wondered what had caused it. The wariness certainly hadn't been there the first time he had met her. She would have seen it. She had been watched by too many strangers in too many strange places not to recognize wariness when she saw it.

Seeing it now so clearly in Rye's glance made Lisa feel suddenly awkward. She wondered wildly whether she should hold out her hand to him for the brief, firm clasp of greeting that was so essentially American. And then she wondered what Rye was doing inside the meadow preserve. None of the other cowhands had so much as set foot beyond the split-rail fence.

"Good morning, Rye," she said, and her voice caught at the hunger that flared visibly when his glance traveled over her body.

"Good morning."

Without realizing it, Lisa simply stood and memorized the features of Rye's face. She loved the forelock that had escaped from his hat to lie in sable profusion across his forehead. The very dark, shining brown color was matched in the steep arch of his eyebrows and in the long, dense eyelashes that were almost startling against the hard planes of his face. His eyes were very light, a glittering, crystal gray that was shot through with tiny shards of blue and surrounded by a thin rim of black. He hadn't shaved recently. Stubble darkened his face, gave it texture and made the contrasting paleness of his eyes even more pronounced. His mouth was wide, his upper lip cleanly shaped and his lower lip just full enough to remind her of the instant of brushing contact when he had kissed her. His caress had been unexpected, firm and soft at once, and his lips had been a teasing resilience that she wanted to experience again.

"Is my nose on straight?" Rye drawled.

Lisa felt a flush climbing up her fair cheeks. Staring was staring, no matter what the culture, and she had been caught with her eyes wide open as she drank in his appearance. No wonder he was wary of her. Around him, she wasn't quite sane.

"Actually, no," she said, rallying. "Your nose looks a bit crooked."

"The first bronc I rode bucked me into next week. Broke my nose, two ribs and my pride."

"What did you do?"

"Breathed through my mouth while I learned to ride. For a city boy, I didn't do too bad after that."

Lisa's shock was clear on her face. "You were raised in a city?"

Rye started to curse his loose tongue before he remembered that many modern cowhands started out on paved streets. A man couldn't help it if his parents had bad taste in living places. "For my first fifteen years. Then my mother died. My dad remarried and we moved to a ranch."

Lisa started to ask where Rye's father was now, then hesitated. Before she could remember if it was polite to ask about a man's relatives, Rye was saying something about the meadow. The change of subject was so swift that Lisa wondered if talking about family was a social taboo among cowhands. But if that was true, why was Jim so forthcoming on the subject of his own family?

Sunlight glancing off Rye's gray eyes distracted Lisa, making her forget what her question had been. She was accustomed to people with eyes that varied from dark brown to absolutely black. The lightness of his eyes was fascinating. Not only were there shards of blue, but in direct light there were luminous hints of green, as well.

"...think so?" he asked.

Abruptly Lisa realized that she was staring again. "I'm sorry. I didn't hear you."

"Must have been the whiskey jack making all that racket," he said dryly, knowing very well that he had been the distraction, not the raucous bird.

"What's a whiskey jack?"

"The mountain jaybird that sits on that bare pine branch near the cabin and waits for you to turn your back on a piece of bread."

"Is that what you call it—a whiskey jack?"

"Not when it steals my lunch."

There was an instant of silence before Lisa's laughter pealed. Rye felt the sweet sounds sink into him as surely as the warmth of the sunlight and the slow caress of the wind. The temptation to take her lips beneath his had never been greater.

They were parted now, glistening with the recent touch of her tongue, flushed with the vitality that shimmered just beneath her skin. It would be so easy. He could almost feel how it would be, the softness of her flesh beneath his palms, the rush of her breath over his mouth, the sliding heat of her tongue rubbing against his....

Lisa realized that Rye was staring at her mouth with an intensity that made her feel both weak and curiously alive. Prickles of awareness shivered over her skin. She wondered what he was thinking of, what he wanted, and if he remembered that single, fleeting moment when his lips had touched hers.

"Rye?"

"I'm here," he said, his voice husky, deep.

"Is it rude to ask what you're thinking?"

"Not particularly, but the answer might shock you down to the soles of your little feet."

She swallowed. "Oh."

"How about if I ask you what you were thinking instead?"

"Oh!" she said, her amethyst eyes wide with dismay. "Er, that is, I wasn't really, I was just..." She tried to look away from the off-center curve of Rye's smile. She couldn't. "I wasn't thinking, not really. I was just wondering."

"What were you just wondering?"

She took a deep breath and let it out. "How

your mouth could look so hard and have felt so velvety.''

The pulse just beneath Rye's temple leaped visibly, reflecting the sudden hammering of his blood. It was why he had stayed away from her after that one, brief kiss.

And it was why he couldn't stay away from her.

"Did my lips feel like velvet?" he asked softly.

"Yes," she whispered.

Before the last breath left her lips, she felt the brush of his mouth against hers.

"You sure?" he murmured.

"Mmm."

"Is that a yes?" He caressed her lightly again. "Or a no?"

Lisa stood utterly still, afraid to move and thus end the moment. "Yes...." She sighed.

Rye had to clench his hands into fists to keep from pulling Lisa into his arms. All that prevented him from grabbing her was his own wariness of the heat sweeping through him, changing his body to meet the elemental femininity of hers. There was no doubt that she had wanted his kiss. There was also no doubt that she had done nothing to return it. He was hard, hot, ready, and she was standing there, watching him with curious amethyst eyes, catlike in her poise and stillness.

"Now that we've got that settled, how's the

meadow doing?'' Rye asked, keeping his voice normal with an effort as he stepped back from her.

The change in him dismayed Lisa. She wondered why he had stopped kissing her, if she had done something that she shouldn't have, but when she tried to ask him, the words dried up on her tongue. He was looking around the meadow as though nothing had happened between them. In fact, it was as though she weren't there at all.

''The meadow?'' she asked, her confusion clear in her voice.

''Yeah. You know. Grass without trees. Meadow.''

Suddenly Lisa realized that she was swaying toward Rye, her breath held, her mind quivering like an aspen leaf. And he was watching her with something very close to amusement gleaming in his uncanny eyes. For the first time she wondered if he wasn't simply teasing her to watch her blush. It would be the kind of joke that cowhands loved to play on the uninitiated, and when it came to being kissed by a man, she was definitely a novice. If it was a joke, it would explain why her heart was going crazy and her body felt like sun-warmed honey, while Rye was glancing around the meadow as though he had come to see it rather than her.

The joke was on her, Lisa admitted to herself ruefully. What was the idiom that the cowhands had used? Something to do with fishing...hook, line and sinker. That was it. She had fallen for Rye's skillfully presented bait and taken it in a single gulp.

Yes, the joke was definitely on her. Unfortunately her normal sense of humor seemed to be asleep, leaving her to flounder on unaided. Then she remembered Rye's question about the meadow. Gratefully she grabbed the neutral topic.

"Some of the meadow grasses," Lisa said quickly, "are growing at a rate of several inches a week. Number five has been especially productive. Yesterday I checked it against last year's records. There are more stems per plant and the stems themselves are significantly taller. I understand that the thaw was late this year. Perhaps number five does better in a cold, wet climate than the grasses it's competing with. If so, Dr. Thompson will be delighted. He's convinced that too much effort is being spent on desert grasses and not enough on the sub-Siberian or steppe varieties. Number five might be just what he's looking for."

Normally Rye would have been interested in the idea that his meadow preserve was being useful to hungry people halfway across the world, but at the moment the only hunger he could think of was the heavy beat of his own blood.

"Boss Mac must be a very generous man," Lisa continued. As she spoke, her natural enthusiasm for the meadow project replaced the cold disappointment she had felt when she realized that Rye had only been teasing her in his own way, like Lassiter with his solemn warnings about flying seeds and full moons. "This meadow would be a rich summer pasture for his herds, but he set it aside for research that will have no benefit for his ranch."

"Maybe he just likes the peace and quiet up here."

Lisa's serene smile transformed her face. "Isn't it beautiful?" she said, looking around. "I was told that Boss Mac loved to spend time here, too, but he hasn't been to the meadow the whole time I've been here."

"Disappointed that he hasn't come calling?"

The sardonic curl to Rye's mouth surprised Lisa. "No, I'm just sorry that the poor man is too busy to enjoy his favorite place."

"Oh, he's busy, all right. So busy that he told me to take over his meadow watching this summer. He just won't have time to get up here and check on things."

As Rye spoke, he watched Lisa closely, searching for signs of disappointment in her expressive face when she discovered that her carefully laid matrimonial trap wasn't going to work on Edward McCall III.

"Oh," Lisa said. "Well, what sort of thing did

Boss Mac usually do up here? Will you need any help? Dr. Thompson didn't mention anything but taking notes on the growth of his grasses, taking pictures, and labeling them, and keeping the daily weather log.''

The clear amethyst eyes looking at Rye revealed nothing. Lisa was watching him, but not with the breathless anticipation she had shown a few minutes before. She was as relaxed and yet as subtly wary as a doe grazing at the margin of the meadow, alert for the first hint of a predator gliding close.

"He just sort of kept a general eye on things," Rye said casually. "He spent a lot of time by the creek. Guess he liked to watch the reflections in the water."

"I can understand that. There's nothing more beautiful than cool, clean water, not even the first light of dawn."

Rye heard the note of certainty in Lisa's voice and looked at her speculatively at her. "You sound like a West Texan."

"I do?"

"Yeah. I was raised there. They love water, too. They have so damn little of it."

Lisa smiled and began to walk slowly toward the next numbered stake. "Sounds like dryland herders all over the world. There's never enough water to go around."

After an instant of hesitation, Rye followed Lisa deeper into the meadow. Her faded jeans looked soft, supple, and they fit the curve of her bottom with loving perfection.

"They must wear jeans everywhere in the world," he said.

"What?"

Rye realized that he had been thinking out loud. "Your jeans have seen a lot of use."

"They belonged to one of Dr. Thompson's students. She was going to throw them out until I showed her how to put on patches. She liked the result so much that she went out and bought new jeans, faded them in bleach and then spent hours sewing patches on perfectly good cloth." Lisa laughed and shook her head. "I still don't understand why she didn't just keep the old ones."

Rye smiled slightly. "Fashion isn't supposed to make sense. It's supposed to attract men."

Lisa thought of the dark blue tattoos, chiming anklets, nose gems and kohl eyeliner that were fashionable in various parts of the world. "It must work. There are a lot of children."

Before Rye could say anything, his breath wedged in his throat as Lisa knelt gracefully, straining the fabric across her bottom for an instant. She took the picture quickly and then rose to her feet once more with an ease that made him think how good her body would feel locked with his in a slow act of love. She had a supple, feminine strength that would mate perfectly with his male power. She would be like the meadow itself—generous, elegant, fragrant, a sun-warmed richness that would surround him, drenching his senses.

Abruptly Rye realized that he was going to have to think about something else or start wearing his hat on his belt buckle.

"What are you going to do after summer is over?" he asked.

For a moment Lisa said nothing, then she laughed.

"Let me in on the joke?" he said.

"Oh, this one is on me, too," she assured him wryly. "It's just that your question didn't make sense to me for an instant. You see, I keep slipping back into tribal time. No tomorrow, no real yesterday, just every day lived as it comes along. According to tribal time, I've always lived in the meadow and I always will. Summer will never end. It's hard to fight that way of looking at the world. Especially here," she added, watching the grass rippling in the breeze. "Here the seasons are the only hours that matter."

He smiled slightly, knowing what she meant. "And the days are just minutes marked off by the sun."

Lisa turned and looked up at Rye with an intensity that was almost tangible. "You understand."

"I feel the same way about the meadow. That's why I come here as often as I can."

Rye's quiet words confirmed Lisa's earlier guess. The meadow rather than her own presence was the lure that had drawn him up the mountain. She sighed.

"Have you worked for Boss Mac a long time?" she asked.

"Tribal time or real time?"

Lisa smiled slightly. "'Real' time. I have to adjust to this culture just as I did to the others. So...have you worked for Boss Mac a long time?"

"I've been here as long as he has. More than ten years."

"It's a long way from West Texas. Do you see your family much?"

"Too much," he muttered. Then he sighed. "No, that's not fair. I love my dad, but I have hell's own time getting along with him."

"You and your boss have a lot in common."

"Oh?" Rye said, his expression suddenly wary.

"You both love the meadow and you both have trouble with your father. At least, Lassiter says that Boss Mac has trouble. Apparently his father wants heirs to the McCall empire and Boss Mac is in no hurry to provide them."

"That's what I hear, too," Rye assured her, his voice dry.

"I wonder why? Most men are eager to have sons."

"Maybe he hasn't found a woman who wants him as much as she wants his money."

"Really? Is he that cruel?"

Rye looked startled. "What?"

"A woman might refuse to marry a man who is too poor or too lazy to provide for the children she would have," Lisa explained patiently, "but the only time I've ever seen a woman refuse to marry a rich man was when he was simply too cruel to be trusted with her life, much less that of any child she might have by him."

"That is not Boss Mac's problem," Rye said flatly. "He just wants a woman who would want him even if he didn't have two dimes to rub together in his pocket."

Lisa heard the tightness in Rye's voice and knew that he spoke for himself, as well. He was poor and very proud. She had seen enough of American life to know that dating cost quite a bit of money; it was rather like an informal "bride price" that men were required to pay before being granted the right to marry. Rye obviously didn't have any money to spend. It must have stung his pride not to be able to court a woman.

"Maybe," Lisa said carefully, "Boss Mac has

been looking at the wrong kind of woman. My father never had money and never will. My mother never cared. They share so many things in common that money just isn't important to them.''

"And I suppose you would be happy living the rest of your life in a skin tent and eating from a communal pot."

The sarcasm in Rye's voice made Lisa wince. He must be very raw on the subject of women and money.

"I could be happy, yes."

"Then why did you come here?" he demanded.

"I was...restless. I wanted to see my own country."

"And now that you've seen it, off you'll go again, following your husband from one outback outpost to the next."

Lisa blinked, wondering if she had missed something in the previous conversation. "My husband? The outback?"

Rye silently cursed the anger that had loosened his tongue. Boss Mac might know about the future love life of Dr. Thompson's charge, but a broke cowhand called Rye wouldn't.

"Since Boss Mac won't be showing up in the meadow this summer, you'll be going back to school in the fall, won't you?" demanded Rye.

Lisa wondered what Boss Mac's presence—or lack of it—had to do with her going back to school in the fall, but Rye looked so fierce that she simply said, "Yes, I guess so."

"Well, it doesn't take a genius to figure out that you'll meet some anthropology type at school and marry him and go skipping off around the world to count beads with the natives." Rye glared at the camera. "You finished yet?"

"Er, not quite."

Rye grunted. "When you're finished, come to the cabin. I'll teach you how to use an ax so that you and your overeducated husband won't freeze to death in the middle of some damned forest."

Speechless, Lisa watched as Rye strode angrily across the meadow without a glance back over his shoulder. A phrase she had heard Lassiter use came to her mind.

Who put a nickel in him?

6

The sound of steel sinking into wood rang across the meadow in a steady rhythm that paused only when Rye bent to reposition the shrinking log. Usually the act of chopping wood soothed his temper, so long as he didn't think about what had made him angry in the first place. With each stroke of the ax Rye promised himself that he would watch his tongue more carefully when he was around Lisa. It was none of his business what she did or didn't do when she left his meadow. She could marry a Zulu warrior for all he cared. Hell, she could marry ten of them.

The ax sank so deeply into the wood that Rye had to stop and lever the steel loose. Cursing, he examined the cutting edge of both blades. It was a moment's work to touch up the edges to lethal sharpness with the whetstone. Then he peeled off his shirt, tossed it onto the woodpile and settled in for some serious exercise. He was careful to think of something besides Lisa while he chopped. Thinking about her had a ruinous effect on his self-control.

Gradually Rye gave himself over to the age-old rhythms of physical work. Swinging the heavy ax correctly required both power and finesse. There was an elemental grace in the repetitious movements that became almost an end in itself. Like the beating of drums in an unvarying rhythm, the act of chopping wood suspended time.

Lisa stood motionless beneath a trembling canopy of aspen leaves just beyond the stream, watching honey-colored chips of wood leap from beneath gleaming steel. Rye wielded the big ax with liquid ease, as though the long hickory shaft and four-pound ax head were an extension of himself. As he worked, sunlight and sweat ran in golden rivulets down his back, making his naked skin glow. The black, wedge-shaped mat of hair on his chest glittered with random drops of sweat. His arm muscles flexed and then his arms straightened and swept down. Steel whistled through air into wood.

Rye twisted, lifted the ax, then brought it down again with a sleek, powerful motion that fascinated Lisa no matter how many times she saw it repeated. She didn't know how long she had stood there watching Rye before he finally set aside the ax, went to the stream and scooped up water in his big hands. He drank deeply, then sluiced his head and shoulders with great handfuls of water, washing away sweat. When he was finished he knelt for a few moments by the stream, tracing ripples and currents with his fingertips. There was a sensual delicacy to the gesture that contrasted vividly with the blunt power of his body.

When Lisa looked from Rye's hand to his eyes, she saw that he was watching her. For an instant it was as though he had been tracing the outline of her body instead of the surface of the cool, rushing water. Warmth stirred within her. It expanded slowly, sending soft tongues of fever licking through her.

With a single lithe motion Rye stood and walked toward her. When he stopped, his body was only inches away from her. The scent of cool water and warm male flesh curled around her, making her breath catch. He was so close that she could have licked drops of water from his skin. The thought of doing just that sent more heat sliding softly through her.

"What are you thinking?" Rye asked, his voice low, husky.

Very slowly Lisa lifted her glance from the diamond drops of water nestled in his thick, dark chest hair to the clarity of his eyes watching her. She tried to speak but could not. Unconsciously she licked her lips. She sensed as much as heard the sudden intake of Rye's breath as he watched her tongue.

"Thinking?" Lisa made a choked sound that could have been a laugh or a cry of despair. "What I do around you doesn't qualify as thinking." She swallowed and rushed on, saying the second thing that came to her mind, because the first thing would have been to ask if she could sip the water from his skin. "Do you think I'd chop wood better if I were stripped to the waist, too?"

She had meant it as a joke, but the way Rye's glance traveled slowly over the buttons of her blouse was no laughing matter.

"Hell of an idea," he said, his voice deep, his hands reaching for the top button. "Wonder why I didn't think of it."

"It was a joke," she said desperately, grabbing his hands. They were hard, warm and had a latent strength that shocked her.

"Take your blouse off and we'll see who laughs first."

Lisa tried to speak, couldn't and then saw the glint of amusement in his eyes. She groaned, caught between relief and something very close to disappointment.

"I've got to stop doing that!" she said.

"Offering to take off your blouse?"

"No! Falling for that deadpan humor of yours. You get me every time."

"Little one, I haven't even gotten you once."

Suddenly Lisa realized that she was holding both of Rye's hands within her own, hanging on to him as though she were drowning. And that was how she felt when she looked in his eyes. Falling and drowning and spinning slowly, held in the gentle storm of the fever stealing through her in shimmering waves.

"How about it?" he said.

"Getting me?" she asked in a high voice.

His slow, off-center smile made her heart turn over.

"Would you like that?"

"Help," she whispered.

"That's what I was offering to do."

"You were?"

"Don't you want to learn?"

"Learn...what?"

"How to chop wood. Why, did you have something else in mind?"

"I have no mind around you," she said. "How could I have anything in it?"

Rye threw back his head and laughed, a sound as rich and warm as sunlight itself. Lisa found herself laughing with him in turn, not minding that it was herself she was laughing at. There was no malice in Rye, simply a sensual teasing that she had never before encountered and could neither resist nor resent.

"I'll get better at this," she warned him.

"At what?"

"Teasing."

He gave her a startled look followed by a smile that made her toes curl. "You like teasing me, do you?"

She grinned. "Sure do."

"It's called flirting," he said. "Most people like it."

It was Lisa's turn to look startled. "Is this how cowboys flirt?"

"It's how men and women flirt, honey. How did they do it where you came from?"

Lisa thought of sidelong looks from sloe eyes, lush hips moving that extra inch, breasts swaying proudly. "With their bodies."

Rye made a strangled sound and burst out laughing again. "Tell you what. You teach me how to do it with my body and I'll teach you how to chop wood."

Lisa had the distinct feeling that the "it" he was referring to and the "it" she was referring to weren't the same thing. She opened her mouth to point that out, only to stop as she saw the laughter lurking just beneath Rye's carefully neutral surface. He was waiting for her to walk into the gently baited trap.

"No you don't," Lisa said quickly. "Uh-uh. Not this greenfoot or tenderhorn or whatever you cowboys call idiots like me. If I ask you what this 'it' is that I'm supposed to teach you to do with your body, you'll ask me what I think 'it' is and then I'll start telling you and you'll laugh and there I'll be with my tongue tied in knots and my face the color of dawn."

"Can you really tie your tongue in knots?"

"No, but I can fold it up at the edges just like Mother could. See?"

Lisa stuck her tongue out flat, then folded it neatly up so that the opposite sides almost touched each other. An instant later the delicate pink flesh vanished behind her teeth once more.

"Again," he demanded.

He watched in fascination as she repeated the process. "I'll be damned. Now I know how butterflies do it."

"Do what?"

"It, what else?"

"Hook, line and sinker," Lisa groaned.

"Sounds like a painful way to do it." Rye ducked and laughed at the same time. "If you push me into the stream, you're going to get wet."

Lisa measured Rye's size against her own and sighed. He was right.

"You're taking unfair advantage of someone who's smaller than you are," she pointed out.

"Clever of you to notice."

"Where's your sense of fair play?"

"I took it off with my shirt." Rye waited for a moment, watching Lisa struggle to control a rush of incautious words. "Let me do that for you."

"What?"

"Bite your tongue. I'd do it very gently. I wouldn't even leave a mark."

Suddenly Lisa couldn't breathe. She looked at Rye with a combination of curiosity and yearning in her amethyst eyes. Then she remembered that this was simply Rye's way of teasing a girl who wasn't accustomed to the deadpan, leg-pulling Western style of humor.

"I'll settle for having you teach me how to leave marks on a log," Lisa said. "Big marks."

For an instant she would have sworn that Rye looked disappointed, but the moment passed so swiftly that she wasn't sure.

"Big marks, huh?" he asked.

"Chunks. Like the ones you get."

Rye's mouth turned up at one corner. "Don't hold your breath, honey. To chop like me you'd have to be built like me." He looked at the pronounced rise of Lisa's breasts and the flare of her hips and wondered how he ever could have mistaken her for a boy, no matter what the distance. "You definitely aren't built like me."

"It's just as well," Lisa said solemnly. "I'd look terrible with a dark beard."

Amusement flared in his pale eyes. The curve of a smile showed briefly beneath the dense shadow of beard stubble. "Let's see what we can do about your chopping style."

Rye held out his hand. Lisa took it without hesitation. The hard warmth of his palm sent a shiver of sensation through her that made her breath catch.

"Ready?" he asked.

She started to ask what she was supposed to be ready for, then decided that so long as Rye was holding her hand she was ready for anything.

"I'm ready."

"Okay." He turned toward the small stream. "On three. One, two, *three.*"

Still holding Lisa's hand, Rye took two long running steps and then leaped the sparkling ribbon of water. Lisa was right beside him, launching herself into the air without hesitation. Laughing, holding on to each other, they landed on the far side just beyond the silver margin of the stream. They were still smiling as they walked to the chopping stump. Rye levered the ax free using only one hand, for the other was still held within Lisa's gentle grasp.

As Rye looked down at Lisa's unusual, vivid eyes and unselfconscious smile, it occurred to him that it had been a long time since he had felt so at peace with himself and the world. Being with Lisa put him in touch with a kind of laughter that he had rarely known since his mother had died so many years before. Lisa had the same ability that his mother had shown, a way of finding joy no matter what the circumstances in which she found herself, and sharing the joy with a smile or a glance or a word, making everything around her somehow brighter than it had been before.

For the first time Rye wondered if it hadn't been his father's search for just that rare quality of joy that had sent him on an endless round of dating and mating which had brought pleasure only to the women who had cashed his checks. It had been the same for Rye's younger brother, who had married and divorced twice before he turned twenty-five. At least their sister, Cindy, had learned very quickly to tell the difference between men who wanted her and those who wanted only an entrée into the McCall checking account.

That was one thing Rye didn't have to worry about with Lisa. She couldn't be smiling at him because of his money for the simple reason that she thought he was too poor to buy a new work shirt much less to pour diamonds into her hands. But she watched him with admiring eyes anyway. That made her smile all the more beautiful to Rye. Not having to question why Lisa enjoyed being with him was a luxury that money literally could not buy. It was a unique, addictive experience for Rye; for the first time in his life he was positive that he was being enjoyed simply as a man.

Belatedly Rye realized that he was standing with an ax in his right hand, Lisa's warm fingers in his left and an unaccustomed grin on his lips.

"You have a contagious smile," he said, squeezing Lisa's fingers once before he released them and handed her the ax. "You'll need both hands for this. When I chop, I hold the ax down at the bottom of the handle. You shouldn't do that. The length of your arm is a bad match for the length of the handle. Hold it farther up. When you swing the ax back, let your right hand slide up the handle. When you swing the ax forward, let your right hand slide down again. But whatever you do, always hold on hard with your left hand. Like this."

Rye demonstrated the proper technique. Lisa tried to keep her eyes on the ax and his hands. It was impossible. The supple flex and play of his back muscles moving beneath his sun-darkened skin fascinated her.

"Want to try it?" he asked.

Lisa barely prevented herself from asking just which *it* he was offering to let her try. When she took the ax, her fingers brushed over his hands several times. The vitality of him radiated through her at each touch, a warmth that was more than simple body heat. Her hands were unsteady when they closed around the smooth, hard shaft of the ax. She mentally reviewed what he had just told her, took a deep breath, lifted the ax and brought it down on the chopping stump.

The ax head bounced once, barely scratching the scarred wood. She repeated the motion. The ax head bounced. She tried again. The same thing happened. Nothing.

"Did I forget to mention that you're supposed to put your back into it?" Rye asked after the third swing.

"'It' is quite busy enough already without having to deal with my back, as well," muttered Lisa.

For a moment Rye was nonplussed. Then he remembered just how many subjects had been covered—or uncovered—by the word *it* so far today.

"It has been very busy," Rye agreed.

"It certainly has. As a matter of fact, it just went on strike. No its allowed. Be specific or be quiet."

His lips twitched with his efforts not to smile. "Right. Here, let's try it—er, chopping—this way. This should give you an idea of the right rhythm and swing."

Rye stepped behind Lisa and reached around her until his hands were positioned above and below hers on the long handle. Every time she breathed in, a blend of evergreen resin and warmth and man filled her senses. His skin was smooth against hers, hot, and the hair on his arms burned beneath the sun in shades of sable and bronze. She could feel his breath stir the wisps of fine hair that had escaped her braids.

With each motion Rye made, his chest brushed against Lisa's back, telling her that barely a breath separated their bodies. The realization was dizzying, like feeling the earth turn beneath her feet. She hung on to the ax handle until her knuckles whitened, because the smooth wood was the only solid thing in a world that was slowly revolving around her.

"Lisa?"

Helplessly she looked over her shoulder at Rye. He was so close that she could have counted his dense black eyelashes and each splinter of color in his gray eyes. His mouth was only inches away. If she stood on her tiptoes and he bent down, she could know again the sweetness and resilience of his lips.

Rye took the ax from Lisa's unresisting hands and sank the blade into the stump with a casual flick of his wrist.

"Come closer," he whispered, bending down to her. "Closer. Yes, like that."

Rye's last words were breathed against Lisa's lips as his arms tightened around her, arching her into his body. She felt the warmth of his chest, the hard muscles of his arms and then the pressure of his mouth moving over hers. Blindly she put her hands on his biceps, bracing herself in a spinning world, holding on to his muscular strength as she savored the sweet resilience of his lips and the contrasting roughness of his beard stubble, and she wished for the moment never to end.

Suddenly Rye's arms loosened and Lisa found herself set away from him once more.

"What's with you?" Rye asked curtly. "You come on to me like there's no tomorrow, but when I kiss you, nothing happens. I might as well be kissing my horse. Is this your idea of a joke?"

Conflicting waves of heat washed over Lisa, desire and embarrassment by turns staining her face red. "I thought it was yours."

"It?" he said sardonically.

"Kissing me," she said. "It's a joke for you, isn't it? But the joke's on me." She took a deep, uncertain breath and rushed on. "I know that you're showing me just how much of a tenderfoot I am and I'm trying to be a good sport about that, because you're right, I'm a total tenderfoot when it comes to kissing. I've never kissed anyone but my parents and whenever you kiss me I get hot and cold and shivery and I can't breathe and I can't think and—and I don't know anything about kissing and—and the joke's on me, that's all. When you finish laughing you can go back to teaching me how to handle an ax, but please don't stand so close because then the only thing I can think about is you and my knees get weak and so do my hands and I'll drop the ax. Okay?''

The tumbling words stopped. Lisa looked anxiously at Rye, waiting for his laughter.

But he wasn't laughing. He was staring at her, hardly able to believe what he had just heard.

"How old are you?" he asked finally.

"What day is it?"

"July twenty-fifth."

"Already? I turned twenty yesterday."

For a long, electric moment Rye said nothing. Lisa stood without moving, afraid to breathe. He was looking at her from the shining platinum crown of her braids to her toes peeking out from her frayed sneakers. The look he was giving her was as intense as it was—possessive.

"Happy birthday," he murmured, as much to himself as to Lisa. After a last, lingering glance at her pink lips, he met her eyes. "There's a fine old American custom on birthdays," he continued, smiling gently at her. "A kiss for every year. And, little one, when I kiss you it will be a lot of things, but it sure as hell won't be a joke."

Lisa's lips parted, but no words came out. She was looking at his mouth with a curious, sensual hunger that was as innocent as it was inviting. Rye saw the innocence now, whereas before he had seen only the invitation.

"No one but your parents?" he asked huskily.

She shook her head without looking up from his lips.

He took her hand, gently smoothed it open with his fingertips and kissed the center of her palm.

"That's one." He kissed the ball of her thumb. "That's two." The tip of her index finger. "Three."

Lisa couldn't stifle a small, throaty sound when Rye's teeth closed slowly on the pad of flesh at the base of her thumb. She felt no pain, simply a sensuous pressure that sent pleasure flaring out from the pit of her stomach.

"F-four?" she asked.

He shook his head, rubbing his cheek against her palm. "There's no limit on bites. Or on this."

His head turned slowly. The tip of his tongue flicked out to touch the sensitive skin between her first and second finger. Before he moved on to the second and third finger he tested the resilience of her flesh with his teeth. He did the same all across her hand, the tender vise of his teeth followed by hot, humid touches of his tongue. When he caught her smallest finger between his lips and pulled it into his mouth, stroking her skin with tongue and teeth, she shivered wildly. Very slowly he released her, caressing her every bit of the way.

"Do you like that?" he asked.

"Yes," she sighed. "Oh, yes, I like that."

Rye heard the catch in Lisa's voice and wondered what it would be like to hear that again and then again, yes and yes and yes as he tasted every bit of her until she moaned the final *yes* and he eased into her untouched body. The thought of being inside her made him clench with urgent need. Feeling the slow, hidden tremors sweeping through her flesh from her toes to her fingertips did nothing to cool the heat and heaviness of his own desire.

"Did you like having my lips on yours?" he asked.

But before Rye finished asking the question he was bending down to Lisa, for he had seen the answer in the sudden darkening at the center of her eyes. Her amber eyelashes swept down, shielding the telltale expansion of her pupils as she turned her face up to him with the innocence and trust of a flower drinking in the morning sun. Her innocence pierced his desire with a sweetness that was also pain. He knew he should tell her not to trust him so much; he was a man and he wanted the untouched secrets of her body, he wanted to caress and possess every aspect of her, he wanted to feel her softness yielding to his hard flesh, clinging to him, sheathing him in ecstasy.

"Closer," he whispered. "Closer. I want to feel

you going up on tiptoe against me again. Closer...*yes*."

Rye made a thick sound of pleasure when Lisa put her hands on his naked shoulders and arched into his arms. He caught her lips almost fiercely, kissing her hard, feeling her stiffening in surprise when his tongue prowled the edges of her closed lips. With an effort he forced himself to loosen his grip on her supple, responsive body. He leaned his forehead against the pale coils of her braids, fighting for control of his breath and his unruly passion.

"Rye?" Lisa asked, troubled, unsure.

"It's all right." His head lifted and then bent to her again as he nuzzled at her lips. "Just let me...just once...your mouth...oh, honey, let me in. I'll be gentle this time...so gentle."

Before Lisa could say a word, Rye's lips were brushing over hers once more. Again and again he savored the softness of her lips, skimming gently, barely touching, increasing the contact so slowly that her arms locked around his neck, pulling him closer in unconscious demand. When she felt the hard edge of his teeth close tenderly on her lower lip, her breath rushed out in a soundless moan.

"Yes," he murmured, licking the tiny marks he had left. "Open for me, little one, want me."

Lisa's lips parted and she shivered as Rye's tongue licked over her sensitive flesh as though it were his own. The shifting, elusive pressure of his caress teased her lips farther and farther apart until no barrier to his possession remained.

"Yes," he said thickly. "Like that. Like *this*."

The gliding, sensual presence of Rye's tongue within Lisa's mouth wrung a small cry of discovery from her. A wave of heat swept out from the pit of her stomach, a fever that turned her bones to honey. She clung to Rye's strength without knowing it, for all she could feel was the rhythmic penetration and retreat of his tongue caressing her. She abandoned herself to the rising heat of her own body and to him, returning the gliding pressure of his tongue with her own, enjoying the intimacy of his taste and textures, lured deeper and deeper into his hot mouth until she was giving back the kiss as deeply as she was receiving it.

After a long, long time Rye slowly straightened. He held Lisa gently against his chest, trying and failing to control the shudders of desire that swept through him. When he realized that the same wild trembling was sweeping through her body, he couldn't stifle a thick masculine sound of triumph and need. She was utterly innocent, yet a single kiss had made her shiver with desire for him.

"Five," Lisa murmured finally, dreamily, rubbing her cheek across Rye's bare chest. "I can hardly wait for six."

"Neither can I. But I'm going to if it kills me. And I think it just might."

Rye saw the puzzlement in Lisa's eyes and smiled despite the clenched need of his body. "You're like a curious little kitten. Didn't your daddy ever tell you that curiosity killed the cat?"

And satisfaction brought it back.

The childhood retort echoed in Rye's head, but it brought him no comfort. He wasn't about to take advantage of Lisa's innocence by seducing her before she ever had a chance to object. His conscience wouldn't let him take a woman who didn't even know his name. Nor would he tell her who he was. He didn't want to see dollar signs replace sensuality when she looked at him.

Yet he still wanted her. He wanted her until he shook with it. But he wasn't going to take her. Sex he could have from a thousand women. Lisa's innocent smile could come only from her.

7

Lisa hummed softly as she worked on making Rye's new shirt. Gray, luminous, with subtle hints of blue and green, the color of the fine linen cloth she was cutting reminded her of nothing so much as his eyes when he watched her. And Rye always watched her. From the moment he rode his big black horse into the meadow until the last look over his shoulder before Devil plunged down the steep trail to the ranch, Rye watched her.

But that was all he did. He didn't kiss her. He didn't hold her. He didn't take her hand or offer to teach her how to use the ax. It was as though those incandescent moments near the chopping stump never had occurred. He still laughed with her, teased her until she blushed and looked at her with hunger in his eyes, but he never touched her. The one time Lisa had brought up the custom of birthday kissing—and missing kisses—he had smiled rather grimly and told her that it wasn't his birthday.

That was when Lisa had realized that not only wasn't Rye going to kiss her again, he was careful not to touch her even in the most casual ways. Yet he came up to the meadow nearly every day, if only for a few minutes. Despite his baffling sensual distance, Lisa instinctively knew that it was more than the meadow itself that was bringing Rye up the long trail from the ranch.

He's just poor and proud, that's all, Lisa told herself as she finished cutting out the final piece of the shirt. *He can't afford to date and he has too much pride to court a woman unless he has money in his pocket. But Boss Mac's party is free.*

Then why hasn't Rye asked me to go? said a mocking voice at the back of her mind.

Because nice shirts cost money, and everyone wears nice clothes to a party, that's why. But this shirt will be free, and he can't refuse to take it because it's just a replacement for the one he ruined chopping wood for me.

Pleased with her logic, Lisa hummed to herself as she set out the simple tools she would use to sew the shirt. Needle, thread, scissors and the skill of her own fingers were all that she would use, because that was all she had. It was also all she needed. She had been sewing clothes of one kind or another since she had been old enough to hold a needle without dropping it. The pattern for the shirt had been taken from Rye's old one, which she had carefully picked apart into its individual pieces. Using the old pieces, she had cut new ones. The only alteration she had made was to add nearly two more inches in the shoulders of the linen shirt, for the old shirt had been cut too small to stretch across the bunching of Rye's powerful back and shoulder muscles when he worked.

What to use for buttons had bothered Lisa. She had thought of asking Lassiter to buy buttons for her, but he came to the meadow only once a week. Besides, she didn't think it would be fair to ask him to spend his free time shopping for just the right buttons for another man's shirt. She had tried to carve buttons from wood, but the result had simply been too rough-looking against the fine linen. Then she had discovered the solution to the problem literally at her feet. Each year the deer shed their old antlers and grew new ones. The technique of shaping antlers into useful tools was very old, far older than civilization. Carving antler and bone was one of the arcane arts that Lisa had learned along with how to pressure-flake glass into a makeshift knife.

As with most primitive techniques, about all that was required for a finished product was time, patience and more time. That wasn't a problem for Lisa. In the meadow she had fallen back under the spell of the slow rhythms of tribal time, when patience wasn't difficult because there was nothing to hurry toward. She had enjoyed watching the buttons gradually take shape. She had enjoyed painstakingly polishing each one and thinking of the pleasure Rye's sensitive fingertips would get from the satin smoothness of the buttons. It was the same while she worked on the incredibly fine texture of the linen itself; much of her satisfaction came from the knowledge that the soft cloth would bring pleasure to Rye while he wore it.

Humming a work song whose rhythms were as old as the techniques she used, Lisa basted pieces of the shirt together for later sewing. When she finally stopped for lunch, she remembered that she had been warming water to wash herself. She tested the temperature of the water in the barrel that Rye had moved to a sunny spot for her. The liquid was silky and warm. She dipped out a pan of water, carried it into the cabin and bathed with the efficiency of someone to whom bucket baths were an accepted part of life. When she was clean, she put on a pale blue blouse that had come from an open-air market half a world away. One of her two pairs of patched and faded jeans had finally worn completely through at the knees, so she had followed local custom and cut the legs off to make a pair of shorts. In August, the high meadow was more than warm enough for her to enjoy having her legs bare.

When Lisa went back outside, she carefully refrained from looking in the direction of the steep trail. If Rye came to the meadow at all today, it would be late in the afternoon. Often he only stayed for a few minutes, asking her if she needed anything from "down the hill," or if she had been feeling well, or if she had any cuts or sprains that might need attention. She would answer no and yes and no, and then they would talk for a bit about the meadow and the grasses and the turning of the seasons.

And they would look at each other, their eyes full of all that hadn't been said or done.

Lisa's mouth made a bittersweet curve as she caught her reflection in the water remaining in the barrel. The time she had spent in the meadow had brought a golden sheen to her skin, a hint of sensual ripeness that had been absent before. It was the same for her mouth. Her lips were somehow fuller, more moist, a rosy invitation for Rye's caressing kiss—yet his touch never came. She would awaken from forgotten dreams with her breasts full, aching, her body in the grip of the shimmering, elemental fever that Rye had called from her very core.

Lisa dipped another bucket of water from the barrel, unbraided her hair and submerged the pale blond mass in the bucket. She stayed outside to wash her hair, knowing from experience that the process was too sloppy for a cabin or even for a tent. She didn't mind the mess. She luxuriated in the fragrant mounds of lather and the clean, warm water that left her hair silvery with life and light. Unbound, her hair was hip-length, thick and very softly curling. She toweled the long strands thoroughly and combed out her hair with steady sweeps of her arm. Then, feeling lazy, she carried her bedroll through the fence and into the meadow itself. There she stretched out on her stomach, letting her hair fan across her back and hips to dry. The languid breeze, warm sunlight and drowsy humming of insects soon made her eyelids heavy. After a while she gave up fighting the peace of the meadow and slept.

When Rye slipped through the fence and into the meadow, for one heart-stopping moment he thought that Lisa was naked except for the hair curled caressingly around her hips. Shimmering with every shift of breeze, her hair was a silken cloak whose beauty had only been hinted at while coiled in braids atop her head. He stood transfixed, barely breathing, feeling as though he had trespassed on the privacy of a nymph who had been shielded until that moment from human eyes.

Then the breeze shifted again, smoothing platinum hair aside to reveal the earthbound color of worn cutoffs. Rye let out his breath in a soundless rush. He knew that he should turn around, run back to the cabin, untie Devil and ride like hell down to the ranch. He knew if he went and knelt next to Lisa, he wouldn't be able to stop himself from touching her.

And he knew that once he had touched her, he might not be able to stop at all. He wanted her too much to trust himself.

So tell her who you are.

No! I don't want it to end so soon. I've never enjoyed being with anyone so much in my life. If we become lovers I'll have to tell her who I am and then everything will be ruined.

So don't touch her.

But Rye was already kneeling next to Lisa, and the silken feel of her hair sliding through his fingers drove everything else from his mind. Gently he lifted the hairbrush from her relaxed fingers and began brushing the silvery cascade of hair. The long, soft strands seemed alive. They arched up to his touch, curled lovingly around his hands and clung to his fingers as though in a silent plea for more caresses. Smiling, he brushed with slow, gentle strokes, and when he could resist it no more he eased his fingers deep into the sun-warmed, shimmering depths of her hair. The exquisite softness made an involuntary shiver run through him.

He lifted her hair to his lips and buried his face in the shining strands, inhaling deeply.

Lisa stirred and awakened languidly, caught in the dream of Rye that had haunted her every time she slept. When her eyes opened she saw the flexed power of his thighs pressing against his taut jeans and the pale delicacy of her unbound hair clinging to his body. She sensed as much as felt the weight of her long hair caught in his hands, a sensuous leash made of countless silky strands, and each strand bound her to him—and him to her. Slowly she turned her head until she could see his face buried in her hair. The contrast of dark and fair, of hard masculine planes and soft femininity, made her breath fill her throat.

Then Rye opened his eyes and Lisa couldn't breathe at all. Passion burned behind his black eyelashes, a turmoil of need and emotion that exploded softly inside her, bringing fever in its wake. She looked into his eyes and saw the truth that she had sensed the first time Rye had ridden into the high meadow and found her trying to chop wood. She had no defenses against that elemental truth of his passion, no defenses against him.

"I tried not to wake you up," he said huskily.

"I don't mind."

"You should. You're too innocent. You shouldn't let me near you. You trust me too much."

"I can't help it," Lisa said, her voice soft, unhesitating. "I was born to be your woman. I knew it the instant I turned around and saw you sitting like a warrior on a horse as black as night."

Rye couldn't bear the honesty and certainty in Lisa's beautiful amethyst eyes. His black lashes closed and a visible shudder ran through his body.

"No," he said harshly. "You don't know me."

"I know that you're hard and more than strong enough to hurt me, but you won't. You've always been very careful of me, more gentle and protective than most men are with their own wives and daughters. In every way that matters, I'm safe with you. I know that, just as I know that you're intelligent and hot tempered and funny and very proud."

"If a man isn't proud and hard and willing to fight, the world will roll right over him and leave him flatter than his shadow in the dust."

"Yes, I know that, too," Lisa said simply. "I've seen it happen in every culture, no matter how primitive or how civilized." She looked at Rye's head bent over her hair as he smoothed it against her cheek. "Did I mention that you're very handsome, too, and have all your own teeth?"

Helplessly Rye laughed. He had never known anyone like Lisa—wry, sensual, honest, with a capacity for joy that glittered through everything she said and did.

"You're one of a kind, Lisa."

She smiled sadly. She had been one of a kind wherever she had gone with her parents. Always watching, never being a part of the colorful, passionate pageant that was humanity. She had thought it would be different in America, but it hadn't been. Yet for a time, when Rye had been near, she hadn't felt separate. And when he had kissed her, she had felt the slow, sweet fever of life steal through her, joining her to him.

Tentatively Lisa traced the full curve of Rye's lower lip with the tip of her index finger. He flinched away from the innocent, incendiary touch, not trusting his self-control. She dropped her hand and looked away. She was too unsophisticated to conceal her bafflement and hurt at his withdrawal.

"I'm sorry," she said. "When I woke up and saw you, and you had your face buried in my hair..." Her voice died. She looked back over her shoulder, giving him an apologetic smile. "I guess I'm too much of a tenderfoot with men to read the signs right. I thought you wanted..."

Lisa's voice faded again. She swallowed, trying to read Rye's expression, but there was nothing to read. Only his eyes were alive, glittering with the fever that he was fighting to control. She didn't know that; she only knew that he had flinched when she had touched him. When he closed his eyes, she saw the rigid line of his clenched jaw, and she believed that he was forcing himself to be kind and say nothing.

She turned away from Rye, only to find herself still bound to him by the shining lengths of her hair caught between his fingers. She tugged very lightly once, then again, trying to free herself without drawing his attention. Gradually she realized that there was a gentle, inescapable force pulling her back toward him, reminding her that there were two ends to the silken leash of her hair. When she faced Rye again he was watching her with eyes that blazed.

"We have to talk, little one, but not now. Once, just once in my life, I'm going to know what it's like to be wanted as a man. Just a man called Rye."

"I don't understand," Lisa whispered as Rye bent down over her, filling her world.

"I know. But you understand this, don't you?"

A small sound escaped Lisa as she felt the sweet firmness of Rye's lips once more. The caressing pressure slowly increased, parting her lips, preparing her for the tender penetration of his tongue. Yet he withheld even that small consummation from her while he rocked his mouth languidly against hers, sensitizing lips that turned hungrily to follow his seductive motions. She said his name, and the sound was as much a sigh as a word. Hearing it sent fire licking over him.

"Yes?" Rye murmured, nuzzling Lisa's soft lips.

"Would you…?"

Her words broke softly when his teeth captured her lower lip. She made a tiny, throaty sound of pleasure, but the caress lasted only an instant.

"More," she murmured. "Please."

Lisa felt as much as heard Rye's laughter. She opened her eyes to find him watching her with an intensity that was almost tangible.

"Shouldn't I have said that?" she asked.

"Say anything you like," he said, his voice almost rough with the hammering of his blood. "I love hearing it, feeling you turn to follow my lips, knowing that you want me. I love that most of all. Having you want me and knowing that it's me, just me, that makes you tremble."

"Is that part of it?"

"It?" he asked, smiling crookedly.

"This."

Lisa eased her fingers into his thick, warm hair and pulled his mouth down to hers. With the same sensual deliberation that he had shown to her weeks ago, she traced the outline of his lips with the tip of her tongue before she closed her teeth with exquisite care on his lower lip. When she felt the shudder that rippled through his powerful body, she smiled and slowly released him.

"Trembling is part of the velvet fever, isn't it?" she asked softly.

Rye closed his eyes and counted his own heartbeat in the violent race of his blood. The thought of making love with a woman as honestly sensual and sensually honest as Lisa nearly made him lose control.

But she was so innocent that he was afraid of shocking her long before he would be able to fully arouse her.

"Will you...?" She touched his lips with her fingertip.

"Do you want me to kiss you?" he asked, opening his eyes, looking into the amethyst depths of hers.

"Yes," she sighed.

"How do you want me to kiss you? Like this?" Rye's lips skimmed over Lisa's. "Or like this?" He skimmed again, then returned to linger. "Or like this?" His tongue drew a warm, moist line around Lisa's lips, between them, inside them, until she whimpered softly and opened herself for a deeper kiss. "Is this what you want?" he whispered.

When Lisa finally felt the moist invasion of Rye's tongue, her whole body tightened. He began stroking her mouth in slow, sensual rhythms that made her melt against him, moving as he moved, slowly, deeply. What had begun as a simple kiss became the sensuous consummation she had longed for. She clung to him, forgetting his warning against trusting him, knowing only that she was in his arms and it was even better than her dreams. When he would have finally ended the embrace she made an inarticulate sound of protest and tightened her arms around his neck, wanting more of his heat and sweetness.

"Shh," Rye said, biting Lisa's tongue delicately. "I'm not going anywhere without you. You're going to be with me every inch of the way if it kills me...every last inch."

He shifted slowly, lowering himself onto the blanket, kissing the silky radiance of her hair as he fanned it out above her head in a silver-gold cloud. Watching her eyes, he stretched out beside her and traced the line of her cheekbone first with his fingertip, then with the back of his fingers. She caught his hand and pressed a kiss into it before biting him not quite gently on his callused palm. His response was a low, very male laugh. His eyes turned the color of smoked crystal as he looked at her mouth and the curve of her breasts beneath her blouse.

"Do you want me to kiss you again?" he asked in a low voice.

"Yes," she said, meeting his eyes. "Oh, yes, Rye. I want that."

"Where? Here?"

Lisa smiled when his fingertips touched her lips. "Or here?"

She shivered when he traced the delicate rim of her ear.

"Or here?"

His fingertip smoothed over the line of her throat, pausing at the pulse that beat quickly just beneath her skin.

"How about here?" he murmured.

The back of Rye's fingers caressed the hollow of Lisa's throat and then slowly slid beneath the collar of her blouse. There was no bra between his skin and hers, nothing to dull the sensation when he stroked the firm rise of her breast and caught her nipple between his fingers. She cried out in surprise and passion and put her hand over his as though to stop him from caressing her so intimately again.

"Are you saying that you don't want this?" Rye asked softly, tugging at her velvet nipple with gentle, skillful fingers.

Sensations speared through Lisa, making speech impossible. She moaned softly and arched against Rye's touch, holding his hand in place on her breast.

"That's it," he murmured, thumbing her nipple and listening to her sweet cries, feeling the echoes of her pleasure tighten his body, filling him with a heavy rush of blood. "Tell me what you want,

little one. I'll give it to you. All of it, everything
you can imagine.''

''I want—'' Lisa's voice broke as Rye rolled
the nipple between his hard fingers, sending pleasure bursting through her. ''I—'' Her voice frac-
tured again.

Lisa gave up trying to speak. She held Rye's
hand against her breast and pressed herself into his
palm, silently asking for more. Smiling, he slid his
hand from beneath hers, ending the caresses that
had flushed her skin with passion.

''Rye?''

''Yes?'' he asked. His fingers flicked open first
one button on her blouse, then a second, then a
third. As he started to pull the cloth aside, Lisa
made a startled sound. Her hands came up to hold
the edges of the half-unfastened blouse together.

''Don't you want me to touch you?'' Rye asked
softly.

''I—I've never—I don't know.''

''Your body does. Look.''

Lisa looked down at her breasts. The nipples
that ached so sweetly were erect, pushing against
the soft cloth, begging to be touched again. While
she watched, Rye's fingers circled the tip of one
breast, then the other, making the nipples stand
even higher and sending sensations spearing
through Lisa all the way to the soles of her feet.

''It will feel even better without the cloth,'' Rye

whispered, smiling as he listened to the soft whimpers he was drawing from Lisa. "Let me see you, baby. I won't touch you unless you want me to. All right?"

Slowly Lisa nodded her head, not trusting her voice to speak. She didn't care what Rye did, so long as it meant that the ache in her breasts would be answered by his caresses.

Looking only at Lisa's eyes, Rye slowly pulled aside one half of the partially undone blouse. With teasing, sensuous care, he tugged the cloth across the hard, high peak of her breast before tucking the loose folds beneath the firm flesh. He saw her eyes half close, felt her shivering sigh as her breast tightened at the first warm wash of sunlight across it. The nipple pouted in deepening shades of pink, revealing the heightened rush of blood through her body.

"Yes," Lisa whispered, moving languidly, arching slightly. "Yes. The sunlight feels so good it makes me ache, but it doesn't feel nearly as good as your hand."

He barely stifled a groan at the sudden hammer blows of need that made him painfully rigid. She was more beautiful than he had expected, more beautiful than seemed possible. Her breast was smooth and full, the skin flawless as a pearl, and her nipple was a raspberry waiting to be tasted by his tongue.

Lisa saw the fierce clenching of Rye's body and the sudden stillness of his face as he looked at her breast nestled among folds of blouse.

"Rye?"

Heat pulsed through Rye as he heard Lisa call his name in a voice made husky by the same passion that was driving him to the very edge of his control. His whole body tightened until he could barely speak.

"You're burning me alive," he said hoarsely, "and I've barely touched you. You're so innocent. But I'm not. I want you so badly that I feel like my guts are being torn out. I want to undress you, to hear you cry my name when I touch you where no one ever has. I want to kiss every bit of you, to lay my cheek against your waist, to trace the curve of your bare belly with my tongue, to taste the smooth skin inside your thighs, to touch you every way a man can touch a woman. But you're so damned innocent, I'd shock you even if I did no more than kiss the tip of your breast."

Lisa tried to speak, but could not. Rye's words had been like caresses, stealing her breath.

"Do you understand what I'm saying?" he asked roughly. "I'm not talking about a few more hot kisses and then I ride back down the hill. I'm talking about lying naked with you and touching you in ways you can't even imagine, and when you're hot and crying for me, I'll begin all over again until you're so wild you won't even know your own name.''

Lisa's eyes widened and her lips parted over a silent rush of air.

''That's when I'll take you and you'll take me and for a time there will be no you, no me, only us locked together in the kind of pleasure that people kill or die for,'' Rye finished roughly. ''Do you understand that? If I touch you the way you're begging to be touched, you won't leave this meadow a virgin.''

8

Eyes wide, Lisa watched Rye. She opened her mouth to speak, licked her lips and tried to think. It was impossible. His words kept echoing inside her, making her tremble. She hadn't thought beyond the pleasure of his kisses. She should have, and she knew it. She was innocent but she wasn't stupid.

"I'm s-sorry," she said helplessly, hating to know that she had caused him pain. "I wasn't thinking how it would be for you. I never meant any hurt."

When Rye saw Lisa's taut expression he swore harshly and sat up in a single, savage movement. Then he closed his eyes, because if he kept on looking at her, he would reach for her, kiss her slowly, deeply, seducing her before she had a chance to say yes or no.

Suddenly he sensed the warmth of her breath

against his hand in the instant before her lips touched his skin. When she held his hand against her cheek and whispered apologies, he felt the trembling of her body and knew that right now there was as much fear and unhappiness as passion in Lisa. The realization chastened him, cooling the fever that had been on the edge of burning out of control.

"It's not your fault," Rye whispered, pulling Lisa gently onto his lap, soothing her with a gentle hug. "It's mine. I knew where I was going. You didn't." He smiled wryly. "But I didn't know I could want a woman the way I want you. It took me by surprise." He brushed his lips over her cheek and tasted tears. "Don't cry, baby. It's all right. I know myself better now. I won't take either one of us by surprise again, and I won't do anything you don't want. You can have as few or as many of my kisses as you like, however you like them, wherever you like them. Just don't be afraid of me. I'd never force anything from you, Lisa. You know that, don't you?"

The words reassured Lisa, but not as much as the soothing, undemanding kisses that Rye gave to her forehead and cheeks, the tip of her nose and the corners of her mouth. After a few moments she let out her breath in a long sigh and relaxed against his chest. He swept up her hair and draped it over his shoulder so that silky strands cascaded down his back. He wished that he was naked so that he might feel the texture as well as the weight of her beautiful hair. He turned his face into the pale, fragrant strands and inhaled deeply, stroking her hair with his dark cheek.

Seeing the sensual pleasure that her hair gave to Rye sent curious tremors through the pit of Lisa's stomach. She remembered the moment when she had awakened to find him turning his face from side to side in her hair as though he were bathing in the warm, flaxen cascade. She remembered a few weeks before, when he had nuzzled his teasing, sensual mouth into her palm, his tongue licking intimately between her fingers, his teeth closing on her skin until she couldn't stifle a moan. The thought of having her whole body caressed like that made her skin flush with sudden heat and sensitivity. The breeze blew and she stifled a tiny gasp at the feather touch across her still-bare breast.

"Lisa," whispered Rye.

She turned and saw that he was looking at her breast rising between folds of pale blue cloth.

"Do you trust me enough to let me touch you again?"

"Yes. No. Oh, Rye, I trust you but I don't want to make it worse for you. It isn't fair that you should hurt when you make me feel so good."

"It's all right," he said, smoothing his hand

from Lisa's knee to her hip to her waist. "It's all right, baby. This will feel good to both of us. Unless you don't want it?" His breath wedged as he controlled himself, keeping his hand just below her breast, waiting.

"It?" she said in a high voice, caught between a virgin's nervousness and the fever that was burning down through her bones to her very soul.

He smiled crookedly. "My hand, and then my mouth. Here. Sipping on you, tasting you, loving you."

He bent down and almost touched his lips to the ruby peak that was reaching toward him even as he moved. Instead of cupping or kissing the sensitive flesh, he blew on her as though she were a birthday candle. Lisa's broken laugh at the teasing caress become a choked cry as his warm palm took the weight of her breast. Yet still he ignored the tight, pink crown, as though he didn't know that it ached for his caress.

Without thinking, Lisa arched her back, trying to close the distance between Rye's mouth and her breast. The world spun as he lifted her, turned her, stretched her out on the blanket once more. He swept up the weight of her hair, letting it tumble wildly above her head, and then buried his left hand in the silky warmth, twisting it slowly around his fingers until her head tilted backward, arching her back.

"More," Rye said huskily.

Lisa didn't understand, but the feel of his fingers kneading her scalp was so unexpectedly sensual that she tilted her head back even farther and rubbed against his hand like a cat. Her back arched more with the motion, tightening her bare breast, making the nipple stand even higher.

"That's it, baby," Rye murmured, flexing his fingers against her scalp, urging her to draw herself even closer to his mouth. He moved in slow motion as he bent down to her, teasing both of them by not quite touching her despite the mute pleading of her arched back. "Yes, higher. You'll like it even better that way…and so will I."

With supple grace Lisa arched her back fully, brushing the tight crown of her breast against Rye's lips. Only it wasn't his lips that touched her, but the hot, moist tip of his tongue. The unexpected caress made her back curve like a drawn bow. His right arm slid beneath her, holding her while his mouth slowly closed over her breast, gently devouring first her hard pink crest and then the velvet areola and not stopping until he was filled with her and his tongue was shaping her and his teeth were a sensual vise that made her writhe with pleasure. Her nails dug into his powerful shoulders as she called his name with each breath she took, ragged breaths that echoed the rhythms of his mouth tugging at her breast, setting fire to her body.

With a swift motion of his head, Rye turned and claimed Lisa's other breast, raking lightly through the cloth with his teeth until the nipple stood forth proudly. His teeth closed through the cloth with exquisite care despite the hunger that was making shudders run through his body.

Lisa's voice splintered as waves of pleasure visibly swept through her. She didn't feel the rest of her blouse being unbuttoned or cloth being peeled away from her skin. She felt only his hot, wild caresses on her naked breasts as fever raced through her. When he laced his fingers through hers and stretched her arms above her head, she arched gracefully toward his mouth, her back a taut curve, her breasts full and flushed with the heat of his kisses.

"Don't stop," Lisa moaned, twisting beneath Rye, trying to ease the throbbing of her nipples against his hard chest. "Please, Rye, don't stop."

The hard thrust of his tongue between her teeth cut off her pleas. She returned the kiss fiercely, wanting to crush her body into his, shaking with her wanting. His lips pressed down into hers, controlling her wild motions, slowly transforming them into the rhythmic movements of the act of love. She didn't protest. She wanted it as much as he did. She had never wanted anything half so much. She felt his hips settle between her legs, opening them. Then he arched suddenly against the hidden center of her passion, and she cried out in fear at the sensations that speared through her.

"Rye!"

"Easy, baby, easy," he said, fighting the urgent hammering of his own blood. "It's all right." He turned onto his side, bringing Lisa with him. For long moments he gentled her with voice and touch and body, phrases and caresses that soothed rather than set fire to her. "That's it, honey. Hold on to me. There's no hurry. There's just the two of us enjoying each other. Just us and all the time in the world."

Lisa clung to Rye while he stroked her slowly, calmly, his voice soft despite the tremors of passion that ripped through him at every shift of her breasts against him. After a few minutes he slowly unbuttoned his shirt, and his breath came out in a ragged sigh when he felt her nipples nuzzle through the black thatch of his hair until they pressed against his sun-darkened skin. The contrast of satin breasts and work-hardened muscle made his erect flesh strain even more tightly against the confinement of his jeans. He ignored the harsh urgency of his sex, knowing that whether Lisa became his lover that day or took no more from him than his kisses, she deserved better in her innocence and honesty than a hurried, nearly out-of-control man.

"You're more beautiful every time I look at you," Rye said, his voice deep and his breath warm against Lisa's ear. He bit her ear delicately, then with more power, enjoying the way she moved toward rather than away from his caresses. His strong hand stroked against her back, rubbing her gently against his chest. "Do I feel nearly as good to you as you do to me?"

Lisa laughed shakily, no longer frightened by the intense, unexpected sensations that had taken her body without warning. She was curious now, restless, hungry to feel that transforming pleasure again. "You feel twice as good. Five times. Nothing could feel better than you do."

As she spoke, she responded to the gentle pressure of Rye's hand by twisting in slow motion against him, savoring the shivery feelings that went from her nipples to the pit of her stomach and then radiated out softly, hotly, turning her bones to honey.

"Do you like—" Lisa's voice broke suddenly as Rye's knee moved between her legs, opening them. The warm, hard weight of his thigh slid upward until it pressed against her softness, rocking, sending a slow, sweet lightning radiating throughout her body. She made a low, involuntary sound of surprise and looked at him with dazed amethyst eyes. The sensation wasn't as sharp as it had been the first time, when he had lain between her legs, yet still the pleasure could hardly be borne.

"Do I like...?" Rye asked, moving deliberately between Lisa's thighs, accustoming her to being caressed. His body tightened hungrily when he felt the sudden, humid heat of her as she was taken by waves of pleasure.

"D-do you like being touched?" she asked, her voice trembling.

"Yes." He bent and kissed her slowly. "Do you want to touch me?"

"Yes, but..."

"But?"

"I don't know how," Lisa admitted, biting her lip. "I want it to be good for you, as good as you make it for me."

Rye closed his eyes for an instant, fighting the urge to pull Lisa's hands down his body until they rubbed against the hard, urgent flesh between his legs.

"If it gets any better for me," he said almost roughly, "it could be all over." He smiled crookedly at her. "Put your hands on me. Anywhere. Everywhere. Whatever you like. I want to be touched by you. I need it, baby. You don't know how I need it."

Lisa's hand trembled as she lifted it to Rye's face. She traced the dark arch of each eyebrow, the line of his nose, the rim of his ear. When that caress made his breath catch audibly, she returned to the sensitive rim, but this time it was her mouth that caressed him. With catlike delicacy she sketched the curves of his ear using the tip of her tongue, spiraling down and in until she felt the sensual shudder that rippled through Rye's body.

"You like that," she murmured.

"Oh, I don't know," he said huskily. "Could have been a coincidence. Maybe you better try it again."

She looked startled, then smiled. "You're teasing me."

"No, baby. You're teasing me."

He gave a low growl when her teeth closed on his ear in a caress that she had learned from him.

"Should I stop teasing you?" she asked, laughing at his soft growl.

"Ask me again in an hour."

"An hour?" Lisa said. The words were a soft rush of air against Rye's sensitive ear. "Can people stand that much pleasure?"

"I don't know," he admitted, "but it would be worth dying to find out."

Lisa's answer was muffled because her lips had become intrigued by the difference in texture between Rye's jaw and his ear. He didn't complain about the lack of conversation; he simply turned his head slightly, offering easier access to the soft explorations of her mouth. Too soon she encountered his shirt. He drew away for a moment, shrugged out of his shirt and threw it aside without a glance. But when he turned back to Lisa, he was afraid that taking off his shirt had been a mistake. She was staring at him as though she had never seen a man bare to the waist.

"Should I put it back on?" he asked quietly.

She dragged her glance slowly up to his intent eyes. "What?"

"My shirt. Should I put it on again?"

"Are you cold?"

The low sound that came from Rye could hardly have been called laughter. "Not very damn likely. You just seemed…surprised…when I took off my shirt."

"I was remembering when you came to the stream after chopping wood. You rinsed off your chest and shoulders and when you stood up the drops were like liquid diamonds in the sunlight. I wanted to sip each one of them from your skin. Would you have liked that?"

"Oh, baby," he whispered.

Rye caught Lisa's mouth beneath his and kissed her, loving her with slow movements of his tongue, both shaken and fiercely aroused by what she had said. Finally, reluctantly, he released her, because he knew that he was right on the edge of his self-control. He lay back on the blanket, his fingers interlaced beneath his head so that he wouldn't reach out to the pink-tipped breasts that peeked out so temptingly from her unbuttoned blouse.

"How good a memory do you have?" he asked huskily.

"I'm told it's very good."

"Close your eyes and remember every drop of water you saw on me. Can you do that?"

Eyes closed, smiling dreamily, Lisa said, "Oh, yes."

"They're yours, every one of them. All you have to do is take them."

Her eyes snapped open. She looked at Rye stretched out before her, watching her with a mixture of humor and sensual intensity that made her breath stop. Slowly she bent down to him, shivering as he did when her lips first touched his skin.

"There was one here," she said, kissing the base of his neck. "And here...and here," she continued, nuzzling the length of his collarbone toward the center of his chest. "And there was a tiny silver trickle here."

Rye closed his eyes as Lisa's pink tongue licked down the centre line of his chest, burrowing through his thick hair to the hot skin beneath.

"The drops went all the way down to your buckle," she said, hesitating, a question in her voice.

"God, I hope so."

Smiling, Lisa continued down past Rye's ribs, smoothing her mouth along the center of his body, testing the resilience of his flesh with her teeth and her tongue. When she reached the buckle she stopped, and Rye was tempted to tell her that the water had run beneath his clothes all the way to the soles of his feet. His breath came out in a rush when she kissed the skin just above his belt, nibbling all along his flat stomach. He locked his fingers together above his head to keep from reaching for her as her soft lips caressed in a random pattern across his ribs, stopping just short of a nipple hidden beneath curling black hair. When she continued on up to his collarbone without a pause, he made an inarticulate sound of disappointment.

"You missed some drops," he said thickly.

"I did? Where? Here?" Lisa asked, touching Rye's collarbone with the tip of her tongue.

"Lower."

"Here?" Her lips caught and tugged playfully on the hair curling in the center of his chest.

"That's closer. Now go to the right."

"Your right or mine?"

"Either way, honey. You'll find it."

Suddenly Lisa understood. She laughed softly. "Of course. How could I have forgotten that water gathered there?"

Rye couldn't answer, for she had found a flat

nipple and was teasing it delicately, hotly, using teeth and tongue as he had on her. He made a hoarse sound of pleasure. When her fingers began to knead through the thick mat of his chest hair, he twisted his torso slowly, increasing the pressure of her touch. Her nails sank into his skin as she flexed her hands, loving the feel of the crisp hair and hard muscles rubbing against her palms. Her hands roamed up and down his chest, stroking him, enjoying the sensual heat of his skin.

In time she discovered that the hair beneath Rye's arms was as soft as a sigh. The ultrafine texture fascinated her. Her fingers returned to it again and again, just as her mouth kept returning to the tiny, rigid points of his nipples until he could bear it no longer. His hands unclenched and pulled her across his body until she was straddling him. Before she could say a word her blouse was pushed off her shoulders and discarded, leaving her breasts completely bare. The tips hardened as he looked at them, telling him that she wanted his touch as much as he wanted to touch her.

"Rye...?"

"Come here, little love," he said huskily.

Slowly Lisa leaned forward, bringing her breasts into Rye's hands. When his warm fingers found her nipples, she shivered with the exquisite, piercing pleasure his touch gave to her. She couldn't control the cries that rippled from her any more than she could stop the fever that flushed her body, heightening her sensitivity. She twisted slowly in his hands while he drew her ever farther up his body. She saw his lips open, saw the hint of his teeth as his tongue circled her nipple and then she was inside his mouth, captive to his hot, moist caresses. With a moan she stretched out full-length on his body, giving herself to his loving.

Rye's hands closed around Lisa's narrow waist, kneading it even as his mouth tugged on her breast. He shaped the rich curve of her buttocks, sinking his fingers into her flesh in a caress that made her bones loosen. His long fingers rubbed down her thighs, then swept back up again and down and up in a rocking motion that made her tremble. He slid his thumbs beneath the bottom edge of her cutoff jeans, tracing the full curve of her bare flesh.

"Rye," Lisa said, then shuddered as his thumbs burrowed farther up beneath the faded cloth.

"What?" he murmured, turning his head so that he could caress her other breast.

"I feel...dizzy."

"So do I, baby."

"You do?"

"Bet on it. If I weren't lying down, I'd be lucky to crawl."

Lisa's laugh was shaky but reassured. "I thought it was just me."

"Oh, it's you, all right. There's enough heat in that lovely body of yours to melt this mountain all the way to its core."

"Is that...all right?"

"No," he said nuzzling her breast. "It's much better than all right. It's incredible and sexy as hell. I've been missing you all my life and didn't even know it."

Lisa's laughter turned into a gasp as sensations streaked through her from the sensuous tugging of Rye's mouth on her breast. His hand moved between her legs, cupping her intimately in his palm, and she stiffened at the unexpected caress.

"This is part of it," Rye said, watching Lisa's eyes as his palm rubbed against her.

"It?" she said breathlessly.

And then her thoughts shattered into a thousand brilliant shards of pleasure with each motion of his hand. She moved helplessly against his palm, sending a cascade of shining hair sliding over him. He shivered at its whispering caress.

"This is the home of the velvet fever," he whispered against her lips. "Can't you feel it, honey? Hot and sweet, hungry and beautiful...so beautiful."

Rye made a low sound as Lisa shuddered against his hand, for the spreading heat of her body answered him better than any words could have. His hands moved and the snap closing the waist of her cutoff jeans gave way, followed by the soft hiss of the zipper sliding down. Gently, inevitably, his fingers eased inside the waistband. She lay full-length on top of him, trembling, saying nothing as she felt the last of her clothes sliding down her legs, baring her to the sunlight and to the man whose eyes blazed brighter than any sun.

Rye held Lisa naked on top of him, soothing her with long, gentle strokes of his hands, trying to still the wild need in his own body.

"R-Rye?"

"Hush, baby. It's all right. I'm not going to do anything that you don't want me to do."

She let out a shaky breath and slowly relaxed against him.

"That's it," he murmured. "Just relax and enjoy the sun while I enjoy you."

After a few moments the sun and Rye's soothing, loving hands made Lisa's uneasiness at being nude vanish. She sighed and stretched sensuously. Soon her hands itched to stroke Rye as she was being stroked, but when she ran her hands from his shoulders to his waist, his jeans were there, a barrier that reminded her that she was naked and he was not.

"This isn't fair," she whispered.

"I'll survive," Rye said tightly, misunderstanding.

"No, I meant your jeans."

"What about them?"

"They're in my way."

There was an electric silence, then, "How shockproof are you?"

"Quite."

"You're sure?"

"Yes," Lisa said simply, meeting his glance. "Very sure."

Rye went utterly still when he realized what Lisa was saying.

"You don't have to," he said, his voice rough with the restraint he was imposing on himself.

"I know. I want to..."

"But?" he asked tautly, reading the question in the unfinished sentence.

"I don't know how. And I want to please you. I want that so much."

Rye held Lisa close as he turned onto his side and kissed her tenderly. "You please me," he said huskily.

He gave her tiny, biting kisses before thrusting his tongue into the sweet darkness of her mouth. She opened to him, drawing him in even more, wanting the mating of tongues as much as he did. Reluctantly he ended the kiss and stood up. He took off his boots and socks, unfastened his belt buckle and looked down at Lisa.

She was lying on her side, her hair flying around her in silken disarray, her pink nipples peeking out from the white-gold strands. The curtain of her hair parted on either side of her hip, revealing a pearly curve of flesh and a pale tangle of much shorter, curlier hair.

"It's not too late to change your mind," Rye said, wondering if he lied.

Lisa smiled.

Watching her, he unfastened the fly of his jeans and peeled them down his body, taking his underwear in the same motion. He kicked the clothes aside and stood with his breath held, praying that she was as shockproof as she had said, for he was more aroused than he had ever been in his life. He wanted her to take the same pleasure in that as he did, but she was innocent and he expected her to be afraid.

Lisa's eyes widened until they were amethyst pools within her shocked face. She saw the violent pulse leaping at his temple and throat and farther down, where he thrust rigidly forward.

And then he was turning away, reaching for the clothes he had just discarded.

"No!" Lisa said, coming to her knees in a cloud of flying hair. She flung her arms around Rye's legs and pressed her face against the top of his hard thigh. "I'm not afraid. Not really. I've seen men wearing almost nothing, but not...not... It just startled me."

Rye stood and trembled when Lisa's hair settled

over his hard flesh like a loincloth of silk. "It?" he asked, his voice like a rasp. "You do love that word, don't you?"

She looked up and saw the humor glittering through the passion that made his eyes blaze and his skin burn hotly beneath her cheek. She knew at that instant that her instincts had been right; Rye wouldn't hurt her, no matter how great his strength or his need.

"This," Lisa said, brushing her cheek over the full length of his erect flesh, "startled me."

"Baby," Rye whispered, sinking to his knees because he could stand no longer, "you're going to be the death of me. And I can hardly wait."

His fingers skimmed beneath the shimmering curtain of Lisa's hair, then curved around the back of her thighs, rocking her up against his body. Her breath caught and held as his fingers stroked down her thighs and then returned to the bottom of her buttocks again and again, each time sliding deeper between her legs, parting them just a bit more with every caress.

"Do you know what it did to me when you rubbed your cheek over me?" he asked, biting her ear and then thrusting in his tongue.

"N-no."

"This," he whispered.

Lisa bit back a moan as his palm smoothed down her belly and his fingertips parted her tight curls, seeking and finding skin that was moist, unbelievably soft. With each gliding motion of his fingers she trembled more. Her eyes closed and she swayed in front of him like a flower in the wind.

"Put your arms around my neck," Rye whispered, sliding farther into her body, preparing her for the much deeper joining to come.

Blindly Lisa did as Rye asked, clinging to him because he was the only real thing in a world that was spinning faster and faster with each touch of his fingers inside her. She felt neither self-consciousness nor shyness at the increasing intimacy of his caresses, for the elemental fever he had discovered in her had burned through everything, leaving only heat and need.

"That's it, baby. Hold on tight and follow me. I know where we're going."

Rye found and teased the sensitive bud that was no longer hidden within Lisa's softness. With each circular caress she moaned, feeling waves of shimmering heat sweep through her until she could hold no more and her pleasure overflowed.

"Yes," he said, biting her neck with enough force to leave tiny marks, teasing her now with the flesh that was as hard as she was soft. "Again, baby. Again. Share it all with me. It will make it easier for you, for me, for both of us. That's it. *Yes.*"

Lisa barely heard the words that wrapped around her, joining her to Rye as surely as her arms holding on to him and his body probing gently against hers. She felt herself lifted and carefully lowered to the blanket once more. Though he lay between her legs, he did not touch the moist flesh that he had teased into life. Her eyes opened and her head moved restlessly, feverishly.

"Rye?"

"I'm right here. All of me. Is that what you want?"

"Yes," she whispered, reaching down to touch him as intimately as he had touched her.

Rye closed his eyes as a shudder ran through his whole body. The feel of Lisa's small hand closing around him was more exciting than he would have believed possible.

"Baby," he whispered, "let me..."

He took her soft mouth with every bit of the fever that was burning him alive. When her tongue rubbed hungrily over his, he eased himself into her body until he felt the fragile barrier of her innocence.

"Rye?" she said. *"Rye."*

Deliberately he slid his hand between their partially joined bodies, rocking his hips slowly, caressing the hard bud of her passion.

Lisa moaned suddenly as fever flared wildly through her, a fever spreading up from Rye's hand

and his hard flesh. He filled her slowly, moving gently, caressing her with his hand and body until pleasure swept through her in rhythmic waves, pleasure so great that it utterly consumed her, melting her over him again and again, and each time she called his name. She wanted to tell him she could feel no greater pleasure without dying, and yet he caressed her still, rocking within her. Deep within her. And then he was motionless, savoring the agonizing pleasure of being fully sheathed within her.

"Lisa," Rye whispered. "Baby?"

Her eyes opened slowly, dazed by the shimmering heat of being joined with him. "I thought...I thought it would hurt," she admitted.

"It did," he said huskily. "But the pain was buried by so much pleasure that you didn't know. Does this hurt now?"

He moved slowly. She made a soft, broken sound that was his name.

"Again," she said brokenly. "Oh, Rye, *again.*" She looked into the gray blaze of his eyes. "Or doesn't it feel as good to you?"

"Good?" Rye shuddered as he buried himself fully within Lisa again and withdrew and penetrated her once more. "There are...no words. Come with me, baby. Take me where you've already been."

He moved in an agony of restraint, holding back

with all his strength. He had never felt anything to equal the velvet fever of Lisa's body, had never known a physical sharing half so deep, had never believed himself capable of anything that approached the intense sensual involvement he was feeling. He moved slowly within her, deeply, his expression both tormented and sublime, wanting it never to end and knowing if he didn't let go soon he would die of the sweet agony.

Lisa's cries glittered through the fevered darkness that had claimed Rye, telling him that she was on the other side of ecstasy, calling to him. He wanted to go to her and he wanted to stay where he was, stroking the fever in both of them higher and higher while a darkness shot through with colors swirled around him, a thousand tiny pulses of ecstasy pricking his nerves into full life, shimmering, pressing, demanding.... With a hoarse, broken cry he arched into her until he could go no deeper, and then he surrendered to the sweet violence ripping through his control, demanding to be released.

Rye's last coherent thought was that he had lied; he hadn't known where they were going. Lisa had taken him to a place he had never been before, wrapping him in the velvet fever of her body, burning away his flesh, killing him softly, fiercely, burning with him soul to soul in a shared ecstasy that was death and rebirth combined.

9

Lisa sighed and carefully pulled out the tiny stitches she had spent the last hour sewing into the fine linen. She had been thinking about Rye rather than about keeping the proper tension on the thread. As a result, the seam was too tight, bunching the supple fabric. Patiently she smoothed out the cloth with her fingers before running long basting stitches down the length of the seam once more, holding the two pieces together until she could sew the finished seam with much smaller stitches. It had taken her many practice attempts on scraps before she had begun to master the trick of the flat fell seams that she had seen for the first time when she had picked apart Rye's old shirt. The neatness of the seams had fascinated Lisa; not a single raw edge could be seen anywhere on the shirt. She wanted it to be the same for his new shirt, nothing unfinished inside or out.

And that was the way it would be, despite the added work such seams made for Lisa. The additional time to be spent on the shirt didn't register as a problem with her. There was no time in McCall's Meadow, simply the brilliant clarity of summer flying like a banner from every mountain peak. Were it not for the growth of the grasses she photographed faithfully every seven days, she wouldn't have had any idea at all of the passage of time. Summer was a long, sweet interlude punctuated by the sight of Rye riding his powerful black horse into the meadow's radiance.

The thought of grass growing reminded Lisa to check her makeshift calendar. She looked up at the windowsill of the cabin's only window. Six pebbles were lined up. Today would be the seventh. Time to take pictures again. Not only that, but sunlight had begun to creep across the windowpane, which meant that it was after the noon hour. If she didn't get busy, Rye might come riding into the meadow and find her working on his shirt. She didn't want that to happen. She wanted the new shirt to be a complete surprise.

The thought of how much Rye would be pleased by the shirt made Lisa smile. He would be relieved and happy to be able to ask her to Boss McCall's dance at last. There had been many times during the past weeks when he had started to say something to her and then had stopped, as though he weren't certain how to say it. She suspected that he was trying to ask her to the dance, or to explain why he wouldn't be comfortable going there in his worn work clothes. The last time he had started to speak to her only to stop for lack of words, she had tried to tell him that it didn't matter to her whether his clothes were expensive or threadbare, it was enough for her just to be with him, but he hadn't let her finish. He had stopped her words with hungry movements of his tongue, and soon she had forgotten everything but the fever stealing through her body.

Remembering the intensity of Rye's lovemaking caused Lisa's hands to tremble. The slender needle slipped from her fingers. She retrieved it, took a deep breath and decided that it would be better if she didn't work any longer on Rye's shirt. She would probably prick herself and bleed all over the fine, pale fabric.

A horse's snort carried through the clear air, startling Lisa. She came to her feet in a lithe rush, only to see that it was two horses walking up the old wagon road from the valley below rather than one horse alone. Even though one of the horses was dark, she knew that its rider wasn't Rye. When he came to the meadow, he always came alone. While he was in the meadow, no matter how long he stayed, no one else came.

The thought made Lisa freeze for a moment,

asking herself why Rye was always solitary. Lassiter usually came with Jim. Sometimes Blaine and Shorty or one of the other cowhands would show up with film or supplies or a hopeful look in the direction of the campfire. Always the cowhands stayed only long enough to eat and check on her before they tipped their hats to her and moved on as though they sensed that somewhere out beyond the rim of the meadow, Rye was waiting impatiently for them to leave.

And Lisa was waiting impatiently for him to arrive.

"Yo, Lisa! You in the cabin?"

"I'll be right out, Lassiter," she called, hurriedly putting the shirt pieces on top of the closet shelf.

"Want me to stoke up the fire?"

"I'd appreciate that. I haven't eaten lunch yet. How about you and Jim?"

"We're always hungry for your bread," Jim called.

Lisa walked quickly out onto the porch, only to stop uncertainly as both men stared at her.

"Is—is something wrong?" she asked.

Lassiter swept off his hat in a gesture curiously like a bow. "Sorry. We didn't mean to stare. You always wear braids on top of your head, and now your hair is all loose and shiny. Lordy, it's something. Eve must have looked like you at the dawn of creation.''

Lisa flushed, surprised by Lassiter's open admiration. "Why, thank you.'' Automatically her hands went to her hair, twisting it into a thick rope that could be coiled on top of her head and held with pieces of polished wood that were rather like chopsticks.

"Don't hide all that glory on our account,'' Lassiter said.

"I don't have much choice if I'm going to get close to a cooking fire.''

"You have a point,'' he said, replacing his hat, watching sadly as the shimmering, gold-white strands vanished into smooth coils.

"Amen,'' Jim said. "Long hair and a campfire could put you in a world of hurt. Boss Mac would never forgive us if anything happened to you.''

Lisa paused in the act of securing her hair on top of her head. "Boss Mac?''

Lassiter threw Jim a hard look, then turned back to Lisa. "Boss Mac is real particular about the health of the people that work for him. He told us to take special care of you, what with you being up here alone and all, and being such a little bit of a thing.''

"Oh.'' Lisa blinked. "That isn't necessary, but it's very thoughtful of him.''

"Beg pardon,'' Jim said, "but it's real durn

necessary. All us cowhands take Boss Mac's words to heart, 'specially that Rye. Why, he must be up here to check on you pretty near every day lately.''

Lisa flushed and looked down, missing the glare that Lassiter gave to Jim.

''The boys and me, we figure he might be getting sweet on you,'' Jim continued, ignoring Lassiter's narrow-eyed look. ''That would be a real wonder, him being such a loner and all. Why, I'll bet—''

''Thought you said you were hungry,'' Lassiter interrupted.

''—we can look forward to seeing you at the dance, can't we,'' finished Jim, smiling widely.

Lisa sensed that she was being teased again but couldn't guess where the joke lay, unless it was in Jim's delight at seeing a ''loner'' like Rye asking a woman to the dance.

''Don't count on Rye asking me,'' she said, forcing herself to smile as she stepped off the porch and walked between the two men. ''As you said, he's a loner. Besides, not everyone has extra money for party clothes.''

''What do you mean? Boss Mac has enough money to—ow, Lassiter! That's my foot you're tromping on!''

''Doubt it,'' Lassiter muttered. ''You already got both of them in your big mouth.''

"What the hell you jawing..." A look of comprehension settled onto Jim's earnest face. "Oh. Well, shoot. What's the point of a joke if'n there's no punch line?"

"The only punch you got to worry about is on the end of Big Mac's fist. Savvy?" Lassiter shot a quick look in Lisa's direction. She was bending over the fire, stirring up the ashes. He bent closer to Jim and said in a low voice, "Listen, hoss. You better stay down the hill until Boss Mac's through with his joke. You spoil his fun and you're going to be looking for some far-off piece of range to ride. What would Betsy think of that, with you two having another little one on the way an' all?"

"Well, *shoot*," Jim said, frustrated. "You hold on to a joke too long and it's no fun a'tall."

"That's Boss Mac's problem. Yours is to keep your trap shut unless it's to shovel in food."

Grumbling beneath his breath, Jim followed Lassiter to the campfire.

Papers were scattered all across Rye's desk. Each one had a small yellow square of sticky paper attached to the much larger white square. The yellow was covered with detailed instructions as to what needed to be done. He squinted down at one of the little sticky squares, discovered that he couldn't decipher his own hurried note and swore.

He grabbed a tablet of tiny yellow squares and began to write.

The ballpoint pen had gone dry. Disgusted, he threw it into the metal wastebasket with enough force to leave a dent.

"First thing this fall, I'm going to hire an accountant," he muttered. "I should have done it years ago."

But he hadn't. He had been determined to handle every aspect of ranch business by himself. That way no one could say that Edward Ryan McCall III hadn't earned his own fortune. Unfortunately, bringing the ranch back from the state of near ruin in which he had found it took an enormous amount of time. Never before had it bothered him that running the ranch left him with no time for a private life. The women who had found their way to his door hadn't tempted him away from his work for any longer than it took to satisfy a simple physical urge. Being with his family had held no real allure for him, either; in fact, listening to his father's long-winded lectures on the necessity of continuing the McCall dynasty had been a real deterrent to frequent family visits on Rye's part.

He glared at the papers and wondered if he shouldn't just pick up the telephone and order a bookkeeper the way he would a half ton of oats. Why bother with interviews and checking references and all the other time-consuming things that had prevented him from getting an accountant in the first place? Just pick a name, grab the phone and walk out of the office a few minutes later with the job done. Devil would be looking over the fence right now, waiting impatiently for his rider to appear.

But Rye wouldn't be appearing. If he didn't input into the computer at least some of the paperwork laid out before him, the ranch accounts would be in such a snarl that he would never untangle them—not even this fall, when there would be day after day after day of nothing but ranch work to look forward to.

Frowning, Rye turned his mind away from the end of summer. He never thought of endings when he was in the meadow with Lisa. There, time didn't exist. She had always been there, she always would be there, no past, no future, just the elemental summer that knows no time. Like Lisa. There was a timeless, primal quality to her that was both fascinating and compelling. Perhaps it was her capacity for joy. Perhaps it was simply that she was able to live entirely in the instant, to give her undivided attention to each moment with him. Time as he understood it had no meaning to her. No yesterday, no tomorrow, nothing but the endless, shimmering present.

Yet summer would end. Rye knew it, although when he was with Lisa he didn't believe it. When he wasn't in the meadow, everything looked different. Outside of the meadow, his conscience goaded him for not telling her that he was the owner of McCall's Meadow, not simply a threadbare cowhand with no past and no future. But when Rye reached the meadow, whatever he was or wasn't when he was down the hill simply faded beneath the incandescent light that was Lisa. Whether he lay with his head in her lap while he talked about cattle and men and changing seasons, or whether he lay deep within her and felt her passionate cries piercing his deepest silences, with Lisa he had found a peace that transcended ordinary boundaries of time and place.

That was why his words stuck in his throat and refused to budge when he started to tell her his full name. Each time he was with her, what they shared became more and more valuable, until now it had become so precious that it didn't bear thinking about. If he told her who he was, he would lose something that was beyond price. She would look at him and see Edward Ryan McCall III instead of a cowhand called Rye. The instant she knew who he was, time would flow in its regular channels once more. That would happen soon enough, at the end of summer, when she would leave and the meadow would be empty once more.

And so would he.

That's why I won't tell her. Either way, I lose.

Each day that I don't tell her is a day stolen out of time. Summer will end, but it won't end one second before it must.

The phone rang, disturbing Rye's thoughts. As he reached for the receiver he looked at the clock and realized that he had spent the past half hour staring through the papers on his desk and thinking of a meadow and a woman who knew no time. The yearning to be with Lisa twisted suddenly in him like a knife, a pain surprising in its intensity.

To hell with the ranch accounts. I need to be with her. There's so little time left.

The phone rang for the fourth time.

"Hello," Rye said.

"Goodness, what a bark. It's unnerving to know that your bite is even worse."

"Hello, Sis," he said, smiling. Cindy was the only member of his family whose call was always welcome. "How's the latest boyfriend?"

"Funny, Bro. Really funny."

"That fast, huh?"

"Faster. We hadn't even ordered dinner before he led the conversation around to my family. I was using Mother's maiden name at the time, too. There I was, Cinderella Ryan, being wined and—"

"*Cinderella?*" interrupted Rye, laughing.

"Sure. A name that outrageous has to be real, right?"

"You've got a point."

"I should have used it to stick him to a board with the other insects in my collection," she said glumly. "They're getting smarter, but no more honest."

Rye grunted. He knew that "they" were the fortune hunters of the world. He despised all such people, but he reserved special contempt for the male of the species.

"Come live with me, Cinderella. I'll vet them for you. I can smell a money hunter ten miles away."

"I wish Dad could."

"Is he at it again?"

"In spades."

"Don't tell me. Let me guess," Ryan said. "She's tall, brunette, 42-25-40, and her major talent consists of getting clothes that fit."

"When did you meet her?" Cindy demanded.

"I haven't."

There was silence, then rueful laughter. "Yeah, I guess he's pretty predictable, isn't he?"

"Not surprising. Mother was tall, dark and beautiful. He's still looking for her."

"Then he should add IQ to his list of numbers," Cindy retorted. "Just because you're built doesn't mean that you have the brains of a double cheeseburger with no mustard."

Rye smiled to himself. Cindy was the image of

their dead mother—tall, brunette, curvy and very bright.

"Speaking of which," Cindy continued.

"Which what?"

"Good question. When you have an answer, you know my number."

Laughing, Rye kicked back in his office chair and put his cowboy boots on the papers. It occurred to him that Cindy and Lisa would enjoy each other. The thought took the smile off his face, because Cindy would never have the chance to know Lisa.

"...my college roommate. You remember her, don't you? Susan Parker?"

"Huh?" Rye said.

"Ryan, brother dear, monster of my childhood years, this is your wake-up call. *Wake up*. You're having a roundup or hoedown or whatever in a week. A dance. Correct?"

"Correct," he said, smiling.

"I am coming to your ranch in a week," Cindy continued, speaking slowly, clearly, as though her brother were incapable of comprehending English spoken normally, "I am bringing with me a woman called Susan Parker. She went through college with me. We shared a room. After college, she made an obscene amount of money smiling for photographers while wearing the most hideous clothes woman-hating male designers ever fashioned. Are you still with me?"

Rye's inner warning system went into full-alert status. "Beautiful and rich, right?"

"Right."

"Wrong. You're welcome anytime, Cinderella, but leave your matchmaking kit at home."

"Are you saying that my friends aren't welcome at your ranch?"

Rye opened his mouth for a fast retort and then stopped, defeated. "Cindy, you're my favorite sister and—"

"Your only one, too," she interjected.

"Will you zip up?"

"Well, since you asked so nicely, I'll be glad to—"

"Cynthia Edwinna Ryan McCall, if you don't—"

"Shut up," Cindy continued, interrupting, her timing perfect.

Rye sighed. "Cindy. Please. No matchmaking. Okay?"

There was a brief pause, followed by, "You really mean it, don't you?"

"Yes."

"Have you finally found someone?"

Pain turned in Rye again, drawing his mouth into a thin line.

"Ryan?"

"You're welcome to come to the dance. Bring what's her name with you if it makes you happy. I'll even be polite to her. I promise."

"What's she like?"

"Hell, Cindy, she's your friend, not mine. How would I know?"

"No. Not Susan. The one you've found."

Rye closed his eyes and remembered what Lisa had looked like asleep in the meadow, sunlight running through her hair in shimmering bands of pale gold.

"Her name is Woman...and she doesn't exist," Rye said softly. "Not really. She lives outside of time."

There was a long pause before Cindy said, "I don't understand. I don't know whether to be happy for you. You sound...sad."

"Be happy. For a time I've known what it is to be loved for myself alone. She thinks I'm just a cowhand with patched jeans and frayed cuffs and she doesn't give a damn. She treats me as though I've poured diamonds into her hands, and I haven't given her one single thing."

"Except yourself."

Rye closed his eyes. "That's never been enough for other women."

"Or men," Cindy said, her voice low as she remembered her own painful discovery that it was her money, rather than herself, that had attracted the man she had loved. "I'm happy for you, Ryan. However long it lasts, I'm happy for you. I can't wait to meet her."

"Sorry, Sis. It just isn't in the cards."

"Won't she be at the dance? Oh. Of course not. She doesn't know who you are. Damn."

He smiled despite the pain twisting through him. "She wouldn't be able to come even if I were able to ask her. She hasn't the money to buy a decent pocketknife, much less something as useless as a party dress. Patched jeans or silk, it wouldn't matter to me, but I'd cut off my hands rather than make her feel out of place."

"So buy her a dress. Tell her you won the money in a poker game."

"She'd tell me to get a new shirt for myself—and mean it."

"My God. Is she bucking for sainthood?"

Rye thought of the sensual pleasure Lisa took in his body, of the feel of her soft mouth and hot tongue exploring him.

"Sainthood? No way. She's just too practical to spend money on a onetime dress when her man is too poor to buy a new work shirt for himself."

"I want to meet her."

"Sorry. Summer will end soon enough as it is. I love you, Sis, but not enough to shorten my time with her by so much as an hour just to satisfy your curiosity."

Cindy muttered something Rye chose not to hear. Then she sighed. "What does she look like?"

"Lassiter told me a few hours ago that Eve must have looked like that at the dawn of creation."

What Rye didn't add was that he had nearly decked Lassiter for even looking at Lisa.

"Lassiter said that? Holy cow. She must be a real world-burner."

"He was more respectful than lustful."

"Uh-huh. Sure. If you believe that, you better have your IQ recounted, Brother. With Lassiter, lust is a state of being."

"I didn't say he was *only* respectful. It's just that there's a quality of innocence about her that defeats Lassiter's standard approaches."

Cindy laughed. "That I believe. Only a true innocent wouldn't know who you are. Where has she lived all her life—Timbuktu?"

"Among other places."

"Such as?"

"She's a world traveler."

"Jet-setter? Then how come she didn't recognize you?"

"Cindy, I'm not—"

"No fair," she said, interrupting. "You won't tell me what she looks like and you won't tell me her name and you won't tell me where she lives."

"But I did tell you. She lives in a place out of time."

"So where do you meet her?"

"There."

"'In a place out of time.'" Cindy hesitated, then asked wistfully, "What's it like in that place out of time?"

"There are no words...."

For several moments Cindy closed her eyes and simply hung on to the phone, fighting the turmoil of emotions called up by the bittersweet acceptance in her brother's voice.

"My God, Ryan. You should be happy, yet you sound so...bleak."

"Winter is coming, little sister. We're supposed to have a killing frost in the high country before the week is out. Summer will be much too short this year."

"And you'll miss being in your meadow, is that it?" Cindy asked, knowing how much peace Ryan found in the high meadow he had let go back to a wild state.

"Yes. I'll miss being in my meadow." Rye's gray eyes focused suddenly on the peak that rose above McCall's Meadow. "That reminds me. I've got to get a batch of film up there before dark."

"I can take a hint, especially when it's delivered with a sledgehammer. See you next weekend."

"I'll look forward to it," Rye said.

But it was the mountain he was looking toward when he spoke.

He hung up the phone, grabbed the bag of film from the top of a filing cabinet and headed toward the barn with long strides. He had a sense of time unraveling faster and faster, pulling apart the fabric of his unexpected summer happiness. The feeling was so strong that he had a sudden rush of fear.

Something has happened. She's hurt or she found out who I really am. Something is wrong. Something.

The sense of imminent danger goaded Rye all the way up the steep trail. He urged Devil on in a fever of impatience, testing the big horse's agility and endurance. When he burst through the aspen grove at the rear of the cabin, there was no one waiting for him by the campfire. He spurred Devil into the opening of the meadow where the split-rail fence zigzagged gracefully over the land.

From the corner of his eye Rye caught a flash of movement. Lisa was running toward him, an expression of joy on her face. He slid off Devil, took three running steps and caught Lisa up in his arms. His hand moved over her hair, releasing it from its bonds. He buried his face in the flying, silver-gold cloud and held her hard, drinking in her warmth, telling himself that summer would never end.

10

Lisa looked at the pebbles on the windowsill. Five. She glanced at the long-legged bay gelding patiently waiting in the aspen grove. The horse had been on loan to her ever since she had bruised her bare foot wading in the stream and had wistfully asked Jim if she could borrow his horse in order to check the meadow fence. After letting her ride for a few moments under their watchful eyes, Lassiter and Jim had been surprised at her skill on horseback. They had also been full of advice on how to treat a bruised foot.

It had been the same when Rye had made an unexpected return trip to the meadow just before sunset that same day, leading the gelding called Nosy. He had watched critically while she rode Nosy, approved her style and told her gruffly that Boss Mac should have thought of giving her a horse to ride sooner. If she needed something, she could ride to the ranch, and if she was hurt and couldn't ride, all she had to do was turn Nosy loose. He would go back to the ranch better than any homing pigeon.

Lisa's glance went from the pebbles to the angle of the sunlight slanting through the windowsill. It was at least two o'clock.

He's not coming back again today and you know it, she told herself silently. *He said that Boss McCall was keeping everyone hopping getting ready for the dance.*

Rye had ridden up to the meadow that morning, coming to her with the dawn, teasing her from sleep into sensual wakefulness with a tender persistence that had made her shiver with the fever stirring in her blood. He had made love to her as though she were a virgin once more, caressing her until she was flushed with passion, then beginning all over, stroking her body until she was wild— and then he had begun yet again, loving her with his mouth instead of his hands, teaching her of a honeyed intimacy that stripped the world away, leaving only the velvet fever of her body and his intertwined.

The memory of Rye's hot, unbearably knowing mouth loving her made Lisa's hands shake. He had made her feel like a goddess worshiped by a sensual god, and when she thought she could bear no more, he had come to her, teaching her that there was no end to ecstasy, simply beginnings.

With trembling hands, Lisa reached for the brown paper shopping bag that she had set out by the door. She had almost given Rye the shirt that morning, when dawn had turned his skin a rich gold and made his eyes incandescent with pleasure. But she had wanted the shirt to be perfect, and she hadn't had time yet to master completely the old flatiron she had found in the cabin's only closet—along with a rusted Spanish spade bit, a broken hammer and a handful of square nails that had to be older than the flatiron itself. Cleaning and using the ancient, heavy iron had tested her patience and ingenuity to their limits, but it had been worth it. The shirt was beautifully smooth now, and the cloth shimmered as though it were alive.

For the tenth time Lisa assured herself that Boss Mac wouldn't be angry if she used his horse for a nonemergency trip to the ranch. The meadow wouldn't be hurt by her absence. All her photos and logbooks were caught up. Surely Boss Mac would understand....

Quit stalling, she told herself firmly. *Rye said that he wouldn't be able to come to the meadow for a few days, and the dance is the day after tomorrow. If I don't give him the shirt today, he won't be able to ask me to the dance at all.*

Lisa took a deep breath, picked up the paper bag
and went out to saddle Boss Mac's horse.

Rye cursed the walleyed cow in terms that
would have made a rock blush. The cow, however,
was not a rock. She was a cow, which was something entirely different. Compared to a cow, a rock
was intelligent.

"Boss Mac? You in there?" Lassiter yelled.

"Where the hell else have I been for the last
hour?" Rye snarled, unhappy at being interrupted
yet again. He had put off so many things since he
had become Lisa's lover that the men were after
him every ten minutes to make a decision on
something that should have been settled weeks
ago.

"You still doctoring that fool cow?" Lassiter
asked.

"Hell, no. I'm making a damn paper doily."

Lassiter looked over the stall just as the cow's
long, ropy, far-from-clean tail swished across
Rye's face with deadly accuracy. The cowhand listened with real respect while Rye described the
cow's ancestry, personal habits, probable IQ and
certain resting place after death in searing, scato-
logical detail. Meanwhile Rye continued swabbing
antibiotic on the many cuts that the old cow had
received when she had stubbornly tried to walk

through a barbwire fence. And tried, and tried and then tried again.

"She sure did take a notion to leave that pasture, didn't she?" Lassiter observed.

Rye grunted and made another pass with the dripping swab. "You want something from me or are you just exercising your jaw?"

"Your sister just called," Lassiter said quickly. "Your pa's coming with her to the party, unless there's a meeting and he misses the early plane. If that happens, you'll have to pick him up in the city. He's bringing a pack of his friends. 'Bout eight, near as I can tell. Miss Cindy tried to talk him out of it. Didn't work, I reckon. Like death an' taxes, he's coming."

Eyes closed, jaw clenched, Rye controlled the impulse to take a swing at the bearer of bad news.

"Wonderful," Rye said through his teeth. "Just wonderful." Then he had a thought that made his lips twitch into a reluctant smile. "I can just see his latest glitter baby's face when she realizes that the dance floor is the bottom of a barn and the band isn't plugged into anything but two hundred years of tradition."

Quietly Lassiter let out the breath that he had been holding and smiled. "Yeah, that should be worth seeing. How long has it been since your pa came up here?"

"Ten years."

"Been a few changes since then."

"Dirt is still dirt, and fresh cow pies still stick to your boots."

"Boss, those things ain't never gonna change."

Rye took a last pass at the cow's right side, then moved to her left.

"The way she's cut up, it'd be easier just to finish the job and barbecue the old she-devil," Lassiter offered.

"We'd wear out our teeth on her."

Lassiter grinned. He knew that Rye had a sentimental attachment to the walleyed cow. She had been the first cow to calve after he had bought the ranch. She had had twins nearly every year after that, healthy calves every one. Ugly as she was, Rye called her his good-luck charm.

"I've got a call into Doc Long," Rye continued. "When he's through stitching up the Nelsons' crazy quarter horse, he'll come here."

"Did that old stud go through the fence again?"

"Nope. Barn wall."

"Lordy. That's one determined stud."

"Some damn fool tied a mare in heat just outside."

Lassiter laughed softly.

Beyond the big, open doors of the barn, someone began hollering for Boss Mac.

"Go see what he wants," Rye said, ducking another swipe of the cow's tail.

Lassiter left and came back within minutes. "Shorty wants to know how deep to dig the barbecue pit."

"What? He's from Texas, for God's sake!"

"Oklahoma. Stockbroker's son. Shaping up into a real good hand, though. Better with horses than anyone except Jim."

Rye sighed. "Tell Shorty to make the hole big enough to bury a steer."

Shaking his head, Rye went back to working over the tattered old cow. He was interrupted six more times before he finished going over the cuts. Between getting normal ranch work done and getting everything lined up for the dance, it seemed that no one could do without Boss Mac's guidance for more than ten minutes at a stretch.

Finally Rye straightened, stretched the kinks out of his back and went to the huge porcelain sink he had installed when he had built the barn. He sluiced off the worst of the dirt and spilled medicine, stretched his aching back again and thought longingly of Lisa up in the high meadow. But no matter how many times he rearranged what had to be done in his mind, he couldn't find the hours to ride to the meadow and hold Lisa once more.

Suddenly, savagely, he cursed the work that prevented him from being with her. He was still scowling blackly when he stalked back down the line of stalls to take a last look at the old cow. He discovered that in his absence she had left a present for him. Muttering beneath his breath, he grabbed a manure fork, not wanting to risk any more infection in the old cow's cuts.

"Rye? Are you in here?"

At first Rye thought he was dreaming. He spun around and saw her standing on tiptoe in the broad center aisle, peering into various stalls.

"*Lisa.* What the hell are you doing here?"

She turned quickly at the sound of Rye's voice. The smile she had on her face faded into uncertainty when she saw his expression. As he shut the stall door behind him and walked toward her, Lisa's fingers tightened even harder on the paper bag she was carrying.

"I know how busy you are and I don't want to get you in trouble with Boss Mac," Lisa said hurriedly. "It's just that I had something for you and I wanted to give it to you and so I rode down the hill and—" she thrust the bag into Rye's hands "—here it is."

For an instant Rye was too stunned to do more than stare at Lisa. Into the spreading silence came Jim's clear voice shouting across the barnyard.

"Boss Mac? Yo, Boss Mac? You around?"

"In here!" Rye shouted, answering reflexively.

Lisa's eyes widened. No wonder Rye seemed so shocked to see her. Boss Mac was close by and she was interrupting Rye's work. She had heard enough about Boss Mac's temper not to want to make Rye the target of it. She looked around frantically, wondering where Boss Mac was.

"Shorty wants to know how deep the bed of coals should be laid an' Devil just threw a shoe an' Lassiter told me to tell you that Doc Long has to check on a mare with colic before he can sew up your durn fool walleyed cow," Jim said as he entered the barn. The change from bright sunlight to the muted interior illumination made him blink. "Where the blazes... Oh, there you are. Shorty swears he saw that bay gelding you gave to Lisa tied behind the barn. You want me to check?"

"No," Rye said curtly.

"You sure? If'n Nosy threw her or..." Jim's voice trailed off into silence as his vision cleared and he saw Lisa standing just beyond Rye. "Oh, Lordy, Lordy. Me and my big mouth. I sure am sorry, Boss Mac."

Lisa didn't hear Rye's response. She was still paralyzed in the first shock of discovery.

"You're..." Her voice dried up. She swallowed convulsively as she looked at Rye's tight, bleak expression. "Boss Mac."

"Yes," he said, and his voice was as hard as his face.

Lisa stared at Rye, trying to order her chaotic thoughts. "I..." She made a small, helpless gesture with her hand when her voice failed her again.

"I'm sorry, Boss Mac," Jim mumbled. "I sure didn't mean to spoil your joke."

Jim might as well not have spoken. Rye stood motionless, his attention focused solely on Lisa as he waited for calculation to replace passion in her eyes when she looked at him.

All trace of blood left Lisa's face as Jim's apology to Rye sank through her paralysis.

I sure didn't mean to spoil your joke.

She didn't notice the cowhand's rapid, silent retreat from the barn, for she had suddenly remembered the first words Rye had ever spoken to her: *You're something else, little girl. If you'll settle for a diamond bracelet instead of a diamond ring, we'll get along fine for a while.*

Now, too late, she knew what that "something else" was.

A fool.

Rye had warned her in the clearest possible words that he wanted only one thing from her, but she hadn't listened. She had taken her loneliness and nameless yearning and she had created a beautiful dream: a poor cowhand called Rye.

I sure didn't mean to spoil your joke.

Jim's words echoed and reechoed in Lisa's mind, haunting her.

A joke, joke, just a joke...all of it, from the first instant, a joke. Rye was Boss Mac, the wealthy womanizer, the man who wouldn't settle down and provide his father with an heir. Boss Mac, who came from so much money that no one in his family bothered to count it anymore. Like his women. No one bothered to count them, either.

Lisa's amethyst eyes went to the brown paper bag that held the shirt she had made for Rye. She could imagine what he would think of clothing made under the most primitive circumstances, clothing that had all the myriad flaws of handwork. The shirt's stitches weren't perfectly even; there were no two buttonholes precisely the same size; the finished shirt had been pressed by an antique flatiron heated on a stone hearth. And the buttons themselves were appallingly unsophisticated.

Color returned in a flaming wave to Lisa's face when she thought of the buttons, no two alike, carved from antler and crudely polished by hand. She looked at Rye with stricken eyes, trying to find words to explain that she had meant well, she just hadn't known who he was or she never would have presumed...

Another realization came to Lisa in a wave of color that surged and faded as quickly as her heartbeat.

No wonder Rye didn't ask me to the dance. He isn't just one of the cowhands. He's the owner of the Rocking M. Whoever comes to the dance with him won't be a girl who has no money, no formal education, and social graces learned around primitive campfires.

What a joke. On me. Definitely on me.

Wild laughter clawed at Lisa's throat, but she had just enough self-control not to give in. She knew with certain humiliation that if she did, the laughter would soon turn into a raw sound of pain. That wouldn't do. She was in civilization now, where people masked their emotions. That was a social grace she simply had to learn. Immediately. Now. This instant.

And then Lisa realized that she couldn't smile and congratulate Rye on his droll Western foolery. She simply wasn't that sophisticated. She never would be. She was like the meadow—open to both sunlight and rain, lacking protection, a haven with no barriers.

That was what she needed right now. The meadow's generous, uncalculated warmth.

Lisa turned and ran until she found herself in the blinding sunlight outside the barn. She raced toward Nosy and mounted with the wild grace of someone who had been raised riding bareback. The horse spun on its hocks in answer to the urgency of its rider, but a powerful hand clamped onto the reins just below the bit, forcing the animal to stay in place.

"Whoa, boy! Easy, there. Easy," Rye said, bracing himself against the horse's attempts to free itself. When Nosy snorted and settled down, Rye looked up at Lisa but did not release the reins.

The first thing Rye saw was her unnaturally pale skin, her face drawn into taut lines. Her expression was that of someone who had been struck without warning and was searching for a way to avoid further blows. She was looking away from him, toward the peak that rose above McCall's Meadow, and her body fairly vibrated with her urgency to flee. He knew without asking that she was longing for the meadow's timeless summer, its silence and peace. He longed for the meadow, too. But it was gone now, yanked from his grasp by a cowhand who couldn't keep his mouth shut.

Rye hissed a single, vicious word. Lisa flinched and tried to rein the gelding away from him. It didn't work. Rye's fingers were immovable.

"I tried to tell you a hundred times," he said harshly.

Lisa tugged futilely on the reins. There was no give. She realized that she wasn't going to get to the meadow's gentle embrace without first confronting Rye. Grimly she clung to what remained of her self-control.

"But you didn't tell me," she said, watching the meadow rather than Rye. She tried to smile. It didn't work. "Telling me would have spoiled the joke. I understand that. Now."

"Not telling you didn't have a damn thing to do with a joke. Not after we became lovers."

Rye saw Lisa flinch at the word *lovers*, saw the hot flush of embarrassment rising up her skin. She looked vulnerable, defenseless. Innocent. But she wasn't. He had taken that innocence from her. No. She had given it to him, hadn't she?

She gave it to a cowhand called Rye. But I'm Boss Mac. Why didn't I tell her?

Swearing at himself and the world, his temper slipping away word by hot word, Rye ducked under the horse's neck without releasing the reins and forced Lisa to face him.

"I don't know why I'm feeling so damned guilty," he snarled. "I had a good reason for not telling you who I was!"

"Yes, of course," she said politely, her tone uninflected, her eyes fixed over Rye's head on the peak that rose above the meadow. She pulled discreetly on the reins. Nothing moved. "May I go now or do you want your horse back?"

Lisa's careful, polite words had the effect of adding a torch to the spilled gasoline of Rye's temper.

"You know why I didn't tell you, so don't play innocent!" he said angrily, clenching Nosy's reins in one hand and the forgotten paper bag in the other.

"Yes. Your joke."

"It wasn't a joke and you damn well know it! I didn't tell you who I was because I didn't want you to look at me with dollar signs rather than desire in your eyes! Why the hell should I feel guilty about that? And before you answer, you better know one more thing. I know that you came to America because you wanted to find a husband who could either live like your parents or had enough money so that you wouldn't have to adjust to clocks and a forty-hour work week."

Lisa's expression became more confused with each of Rye's words. Seeing that didn't improve his temper.

"You weren't raised to live in the real world and you know it," he said roughly. "Tribal time just doesn't fit in twentieth-century America. So you went head-hunting a rich man or an anthropologist and you ended up giving yourself to me despite the fact that I was poor and sure as hell wasn't bent on studying Stone Age natives. I took what you offered and never promised you one damn thing in the way of marriage or anything else. So you can just drop the wounded-innocent routine. You knew that summer would end and so did I, and then you would ride down the hill into the arms of that jackass anthropologist Ted Thompson has all picked out for you."

Rye didn't ask himself why even thinking about the unknown man waiting for Lisa made his own body tighten in a killing rage. He didn't ask himself about the meaning of anything that he was feeling—he was too angry at sensing summer slip through his clenched fists as irretrievably as sunlight sliding into night. He needed Lisa's sweet fire and shimmering warmth. He needed it as much as he needed air; and he was fighting for it in just the same way as he would fight for air, no holds barred, no quarter given, no questions asked or answered, nothing of softness in him.

And he was losing anyway. Losing her. He had known he would, but he hadn't known it would come this soon and hurt this much. The pain enraged him, and the loss.

He felt the reins being tugged slowly from his clenched hand.

"No!" he snarled, tightening his grip. "Talk to me, damn it! Don't just ride out of here like I don't exist!"

The demand penetrated Lisa's single-minded determination to escape. For the first time she looked directly at Rye.

He had expected to see calculation and money dreams in her eyes. He saw nothing but the same darkness that he felt expanding through his own soul. Pain and loss and grief, but not anger.

The lack of anger baffled Rye until Lisa began to speak. The very care with which she chose her words, the ruthless neutrality of her voice, the slow trembling of her body—each told him that she was stretched almost beyond endurance. She wasn't angry because she couldn't afford to be without losing all control over herself.

"I don't know anything about an anthropologist, jackass or otherwise," Lisa said. "My parents sent me here to find a husband, but that's not why I came. I wanted to find out who and what I am. I didn't fit into any of the cultures I grew up in. I was always the white, skinny outsider, too aware of other traditions, other gods, other ways to live. I thought I must belong here, in America, where people come in all colors and traditions are something families invent as they go along. I was wrong. I don't belong here. I'm too...poor."

"That doesn't say anything about us, about you and me," Rye countered coolly.

Lisa closed her eyes as pain twisted through her, leaving her shaken. "What do you mean?"

"You're hurt and upset because I fooled you, and right now I'm mad as hell at everyone involved, including myself. But underneath it all nothing has changed between us. I look at you and I want you so bad I can hardly stand up. You look at me and it's the same. We're a fever in each other's blood. That hasn't changed."

Lisa looked at Rye, at the hard line of his mouth and the blazing gray of his eyes, and knew that he was right. Even now, with anger and pain churning inside her, she could look at him and want him until she was dizzy with it.

Fever.

Rye saw the answering desire in Lisa's eyes and felt as though the claws that had been twisting in his guts were being slowly withdrawn. The end of summer would come...but not today. Not this instant. He could breathe again. He let out a long, harsh breath and released the reins, transferring his hand to the worn softness of the fabric stretched across Lisa's thigh.

"There's one good thing to come out of this mess," he said roughly. "Now that you know who I am, there's no reason you can't come to the dance."

As soon as Rye mentioned the dance, Lisa remembered the wretched shirt concealed within the bag he still held. Suddenly she knew that she could survive anything but him looking at that shirt and seeing all of her shortcomings so painfully revealed.

"Thank you, that's very kind of you," Lisa said quickly, "but I don't know how to dance."

She smiled at him, silently pleading that he understand that it wasn't anger or pride which made her refuse. She was out of place down here, and she knew it.

But Rye wasn't in an understanding mood.

From the front of the barn came Lassiter's voice

calling for Boss Mac. Rye swore viciously under his breath.

"I'll teach you how to dance," he said flatly.

She shook her head slowly, unable to speak.

"Yes," he countered.

"Yo! Boss Mac! You in the barn?" yelled Lassiter, his voice fading as he went into the barn. "You got a call from Houston waiting on..."

"You'd better go," Lisa said, gently pulling on the reins again.

Rye lifted his hand from her thigh and held on to the reins. "Not until you agree to come to the dance."

"Boss Mac? Yo! Boss Mac! Where in hell are you!"

"I don't think that would be a good idea," Lisa said hurriedly. "I really don't know anything about American customs or—"

"Shove customs," Rye snarled. "I'm asking you to a dance, not to take notes about quaint native practices!"

"Boss Mac! Yo!"

"I'm coming, damn it!"

The horse shied nervously at Rye's bellow. He simply clamped down harder on the reins and glared up at Lisa.

"You're coming to the dance," he said flatly. "If you don't have a party dress, I'll get you one."

"No," she said quickly, remembering all too

well his comment about giving her a diamond bracelet if she pleased him. "No dress. No diamond bracelet. Nothing. I have everything I need."

Rye started to argue, but a single look at Lisa's pale, set expression told him that it would be useless.

"Fine," he said in a taut voice. "Wear your damn jeans. It doesn't matter to me. If you don't want to dance we'll just listen to the music. That doesn't require anything but ears, and you damn well have two of them. I won't have time to come up to the cabin and get you. I've spent too many hours away from here in the past weeks. If I don't get to work, there won't *be* a dance—or a ranch, either, for that matter."

Lisa smiled sadly as she saw Lassiter approaching from one direction and Jim coming at a trot from another, men descending on Rye like flies on honey. The thought of how much time he had stolen from his work to be with her was both soothing and disturbing. Rye might have had that kind of time to spare; Boss Mac obviously did not.

"I'll send Lassiter for you tomorrow afternoon," Rye said. "Early."

Hesitantly, knowing that it was a mistake, Lisa nodded her head. She could no more resist seeing Rye again than water could resist running downhill.

Relief swept through Rye, an emotion so powerful that he nearly sagged beneath its weight. He looked up searchingly at Lisa, trying to see beyond the shadows in her eyes to the warmth and laughter that had always been beneath.

"Baby?" he said softly, tracing Lisa's thigh with his knuckles while he held on to the paper bag. "I'm sorry that I didn't tell you sooner. I just didn't want things to…change."

Lisa nodded again and touched Rye's hand lightly. When one of his fingers reached to curl around her own, she removed the paper bag from his grip, squeezed his hand and simultaneously tugged on the reins, freeing them from his grasp. By the time he realized that the bag was in her hands, Nosy had backed up beyond his reach.

"Lisa?"

She looked at him, her face pale, her eyes so dark that no color showed.

"Didn't you ride all the way down the hill to give me that bag?"

She shook her head and tried to make her voice light. "This was for a cowboy called Rye. He lives in the meadow. Boss Mac lives down here."

Rye felt the cold claws sliding into his guts once more. "Rye and Boss Mac are the same man."

Lisa reined the horse toward the mountains without answering.

"Lisa?" Rye called. "Lisa! What did you want to give me?"

The answer came back to him, carried on the wind sweeping down from the high peaks.

"Nothing you need...."

Rye stood for a long time, hearing the words echo in his mind. He sensed something sliding through his grasp, something retreating from him. He told himself that he was being foolish; Lisa had been shocked and hurt and she had taken back whatever present she had intended to give him, but she was coming to the dance with him. He would see her again. Summer hadn't ended yet.

Nothing you need....

Suddenly he sensed an abyss opening beneath the casual words, a feeling that he had lost something he could not name.

"Nothing has changed," he told himself fiercely. "She still wants me and there's no money attached to it. Nothing has changed!"

But he didn't believe that, either.

11

The morning of the dance, Lisa awoke to an un-earthly landscape of glittering diamond dust and a sky of radiant sapphire. Aspen leaves shivered in brilliant shades of citrine that made nearby ever-greens appear almost black by contrast. Lisa's breath was a silver cloud and the air itself was so cold and pure that it shone as though polished. She stood in the cabin's open door and drank the meadow's beauty until her own shivering could no longer be ignored.

Only once did she think of Rye, who was Boss Mac, who was not Rye.

No. Don't think about it. There's nothing I can do to change what happened any more than I can run back through the night into yesterday's warmth. I have to be like the aspens. They would love to have the sweet fever of summer forever, yet they aren't angry at its end. They save their

*greatest beauty for the final, bittersweet moments
of their summer affair.*

And so will I. Somehow.

The jeans that Lisa pulled on were stiff with
cold and patched in as many colors as the morning
itself. She finished dressing quickly in a T-shirt,
blouse, sweatshirt, wind-shell, socks and shoes, all
but emptying out the closet.

Outside, the sunlight was so bright that the
campfire's flames were invisible but for the subtle
distortion of the heat waves rising into the intense
blue of the sky. The coffee smelled like heaven
and tasted even better as it spread through Lisa's
chilled body. The contrast between cold and heat,
frost and fire, heightened all her senses. Suspended
like the aspens between the season of fire and the
coming of ice, she watched in rapt silence while
frost crystals sparkled and vanished as shade retreated across the meadow before the still-
powerful sun.

When the final gleaming hints of frost had gone
and all the plants were dry, Lisa slipped through
the meadow fence with the camera in her hand. It
would be the last time she recorded the height of
plants against their numbered stakes, for the frost
had been as hard as it had been beautiful; it had
brought the end of growth in its glittering wake.

The meadow had not been taken by surprise. It
had been preparing for that diamond-bright morn-

ing since the first tender shoots of new growth had unfurled beneath melting spring snow months before. The feverish rush of summer had already come to fruition. Grasses nodded and bowed to each passing breeze, their plumed, graceful heads heavy with the seeds of the next summer's growth. Beyond the grasses, aspens trembled and burned, their leaves such a pure, vivid yellow that Lisa could not bear to look at it without narrowing her eyes.

She moved through the meadow with the silence and ease of a wild thing. Her hands were light, quick and sure as she cut seed heads from grasses, taking only what Dr. Thompson needed from each plant and leaving the rest for the meadow and its creatures. Back at the cabin she sorted the numbered collection bags and set them aside. She pasted the pictures she had just taken into the log, entered the necessary comments and put the notebook aside, as well.

The angle of the sunlight and Lisa's growling stomach told her that it was past noon. The realization yanked her from the tribal time into which she had retreated, letting its slow, elemental rhythms soothe the turmoil inside her. She ate a cold lunch while she heated water for washing her hair. Long before the smoke-blackened bucket began to steam, she heard hoofbeats. Her heart beat wildly, but when she turned around it was only Lassiter.

What did I expect? Rye—Boss Mac—said he would send Lassiter, and that's just what he did.

"Hello," Lisa said, smiling through stiff lips. "Have you eaten lunch?"

"Afraid so," Lassiter said regretfully. "Boss Mac didn't want me to fool around up here before I brought you down the hill. Then just as I was leaving his pa called. The boss had to drive all the way into the city to pick him up. I'll tell you true, Miss Lisa, by the time Boss Mac gets back this evening, he'll be in a temper that would shame a broken-toothed grizzly."

"I see. Well, pour yourself a cup of coffee anyway while I get some things from the cabin. I won't tell Boss Mac we took a few extra minutes of his time if you won't."

Lassiter swung down from his horse and walked toward Lisa. His eyes searched her face. "You feeling okay?"

"I'm fine, thank you. And no, I didn't cut myself or sprain anything, and I don't need supplies or film from down the hill," she added, forcing herself to smile as she went through the familiar list.

Lassiter smiled in return, even though his question hadn't been meant as part of the quiz Boss Mac administered to any cowhand who had seen

Lisa. Lassiter watched Lisa closely while she put out the small campfire with a thoroughness that spoke of long practice. He sensed something different about her, but he couldn't decide just what it was.

"I see you got a good frost last night," he said finally, looking from the blazing yellow aspens to the deceptively green meadow.

"Yes," Lisa said.

"It will stay hot for a few days more, though."

"Will it? How can you tell?"

"The wind shifted late this morning. It's from the south now. Guess we're going to have an Indian summer."

"What's that?" Lisa asked.

"Sort of a grace period between the first killing frost and the beginning of real cold. All the blessings of summer and no bugs."

Lisa looked toward the aspens. "False summer," she murmured, "and all the sweeter for it. The aspens know. They're wearing their brightest smiles."

She ran quickly to the cabin and emerged a few moments later carrying her backpack, her braided hair hidden beneath a bright scarf tied at the nape of her neck. Lassiter had saddled and bridled Nosy for her while she was in the cabin. As he handed over the reins, he looked at Lisa and realized what had been missing. There was no laughter in her today, but yesterday laughter had been as much a part of Lisa as her matchless violet eyes.

"He didn't mean no harm," Lassiter said quietly.

She turned toward him, confused, for her mind had been with the transformed aspen leaves burning like thousands of candle flames against the intense blue of the autumn sky.

"Boss Mac," Lassiter explained. "Oh, he's got a temper on him sure enough, and he won't back up for man nor beast, but he's not small-minded or vicious. He didn't mean for his joke to hurt you."

Lisa smiled very carefully, very brightly, her eyes reflecting the blazing meadow aspens. "I'm sure he didn't. If I haven't laughed in all the right places, don't worry. I just don't understand all the fine points of Western humor yet."

"You're sweet on him, aren't you?" Lassiter said quietly.

Her face became expressionless. "Boss Mac?"

Lassiter nodded.

"No," she said, reining the gelding toward the wagon trail. "I was 'sweet on' a cowhand called Rye."

For a moment Lassiter simply stood with his mouth open, staring at Lisa as she rode away. Then he mounted quickly and followed her out of the meadow. All the way down to the ranch he was careful to keep the conversation on Jim's teething baby, Shorty's barbecue pit and the wall-eyed cow that had more stitches in her hide than a pair of hand-tooled boots. Though Lisa still smiled far too little to suit Lassiter, she was more like herself by the end of the ride, and if sometimes her smile didn't match the shadows in her eyes, he saw no need to make an issue out of it.

When Lisa and Lassiter rode into the yard, there were expensive cars parked every which way, their paint gleaming like colored water beneath a coating of dust from the rough ranch road. There were battered pickups from nearby ranches, plus several strange horses in the corral. A big, candy-striped awning stretched down one side of the barn, protecting long tables from the afternoon thundershowers that often rumbled down from the mountain peaks. People shouted greetings and called to one another as they carried huge, covered dishes from their cars to the ranch kitchen. Everyone seemed to know everyone else.

A familiar feeling came back to Lisa, a combination of wistfulness and uneasiness that came from being the one who didn't belong at the gathering of clans. Welcome—yes. But a member of the tribe? No.

"Well, I see the Leighton kids came in over High Pass the way they used to 'fore the state highway come through," Lassiter said.

Lisa followed his glance to the corral, where three strange horses lipped hay from a small mound that had been dropped over the rails. "High Pass?"

"The trail you asked about just before we crossed the first stream and after Boss Mac's short-cut comes into the wagon road. The trail goes out over the mountain to the Leighton place. From there it's only a mile or two into town." Lassiter scanned the parked vehicles again and swore beneath his breath. "I don't see Boss Mac's pickup. That means his pa missed the early plane. Hellfire and damnation," Lassiter said, sighing and pulling his hat into place with a sharp motion of his hand. "The boss will be chewing nails and spitting tacks, no two ways about it. C'mon, let's get you settled so he won't have that to jaw at me about."

"Settled?"

"Boss Mac said for you to put your gear in his room." Lassiter spoke casually, looking anywhere but at the sudden rush of color on Lisa's face. "It's the big one just off the living room. His sister and her friend and his pa and his friends will take over the rest of the place," Lassiter continued hurriedly, "so there wasn't much choice."

"No problem," Lisa said tightly. "I won't be staying the night, so I'll need the room only long enough to wash up and change clothes."

"But Boss Mac said—"

"Shall I put Nosy in the corral or the pasture?" Lisa interrupted, her words crisp.

The thought that Rye—no, not Rye, *Boss Mac*—had assumed that she would calmly move into his bedroom infuriated Lisa. For the first time since she had discovered who Rye really was, she felt not only sad and foolish but insulted, as well. She could accept the end of summer without real anger, for living among various tribes had taught her that the passage of seasons was as inevitable as the progression from light to dark and back to light again.

But she could not accept becoming the latest of Boss Mac's women.

"I'll put Nosy in the barn," Lassiter said, watching Lisa warily, seeing the anger that had replaced the first flush of humiliation. "He could use some oats after being on grass for the last few weeks."

"Thank you," she said, dismounting. "Will you leave the tack on the stall door?"

"He told me to put it away. He told me you wouldn't be needing it anymore, or the horse, neither." Lassiter cleared his throat and added uncomfortably, "It's pretty plain that Boss Mac expects you to stay here."

"In his bedroom?" Lisa inquired, raising one platinum eyebrow in an elegant arc. "With him? That's not very likely, is it? I just met the man yesterday. He must have me confused with one of his other women.''

Lassiter opened his mouth, closed it and smiled reluctantly. ''He didn't say nothing about where *he* was planning to sleep. Just where he was planning for *you* to sleep. He's never had a woman here overnight. Not once.''

''Good heavens. I certainly wouldn't want to spoil his spotless record. Especially on such short acquaintance.''

Slowly Lassiter's smile dissolved into laughter. He leaned over the saddle horn and looked at Lisa admiringly. ''Guess you're gonna get some of your own back, huh?''

''I'm going to what?''

''Get even,'' he said succinctly.

The idea hadn't occurred to Lisa in just those terms. Once it had, the temptation was very real. Then she thought of the aspens burning silently, each yellow leaf a proclamation both of the summer's bounty and the end of heat. She had no more chance to beat Rye at his own game than the aspens had of staying green through winter.

Lisa dismounted, resettled her backpack and went into the house as Lassiter led Nosy away. Even to her uncritical eye, the ranch house's furnishings were Spartan, with the exception of the office. There was nothing spare, worn or second-rate about the computer, just as there was nothing cheap about the cattle, the horses or the wages of the men who worked for Boss Mac.

I wonder what he pays his women?

The answer to that unhappy thought came as quickly as the question had.

Diamond bracelets, of course.

There was no doubt as to which bedroom was Rye's. It was the only one with a bed big enough for him. Attached to the bedroom was a bathroom with an oversized shower. Lisa shot the bolt of the bedroom door behind her. She removed the length of amethyst cloth from her backpack, shook out the long piece of linen and hung it over a hanger in the bathroom. She took a long, luxuriant shower, relishing every hot drop of water, feeling like a queen in a palace bath. When she finally emerged from the shower, the steam had removed most of the wrinkles in the linen. The rest succumbed to the small iron she found in Rye's closet.

After a few tries she got the knack of the bright pink blow-dryer that had been left out on the bathroom counter. She couldn't imagine Rye using the device any more than she could imagine him using the scented soap and shampoo that had been in the shower. She almost hadn't used them herself, because the bottles had been unopened.

Maybe Rye brought women here more often than Lassiter thought.

Unhappily Lisa brushed her hair until it was a fragrant, silver-gold cloud clinging to everything it touched. She outlined her eyes in the manner of Middle Eastern women since the dawn of time. Mascara made her long amber lashes as dark as the center of her eyes. She colored her lips from the glossy contents of a fragrant wooden pot no bigger than her thumb. The scent she used was a mixture of rose petals and musk that was as ancient in cosmetic lineage as the kohl lining her eyes.

She gathered the silky wildness of her hair and wove it into a gleaming, intricate mass, which she secured on top of her head with two long ebony picks. The picks were inlaid with iridescent bits of seashell, as were the six ebony bracelets she put on her left wrist. Slipper-shoes of glittery black went from the backpack to her feet. She picked up the rich amethyst strip of linen and began winding it around herself in the manner of an Indian sari. The last four feet of the radiant cloth formed a loose covering over her hair and made her eyes look like huge amethyst gems set in skin as fine grained and luminous as pearl.

"Lisa? Are you in there? Open up. I have to take a shower and Cindy's camped in the other bathroom."

Lisa jumped at the unexpected sound of Rye's voice. Her heart went wild.

That can't be Rye. It's too soon.

A quick glance out the bedroom window told Lisa that the afternoon had indeed slipped away. She started toward the bedroom door, only to stop as her hand touched the bolt. She wasn't ready to face Rye and smile as brightly as the meadow aspens. She wasn't sure that she would ever be that brave.

"Lisa? I know you're in there. Open the damned door!"

Before she could speak, Lassiter's familiar cry rang through the house.

"Boss Mac? Yo, Boss Mac! You in the house? Blaine says that walleyed cow is chewing out her stitches. You want to call the doc again or you want to sew up the old she-devil yourself?"

What Rye said in response convinced Lisa that Lassiter had been correct; right now Rye was in a mood to give a sore-toothed bear lessons in how to be obnoxious. She heard his boot heels punctuate every one of his strides between the bedroom and the front door. When the sound of his swearing faded, she peeked out, saw no one and hurriedly left the bedroom. As she rounded the corner into the living room, she nearly ran into a tall, slender woman who had hair the color of freshly ground cinnamon, the carriage of a queen or a model—and a very expensive diamond bracelet on her elegant wrist.

"My God," the woman said, staring at Lisa. "Since when did Ryan start keeping a harem?"

"Ryan?"

"McCall. As in Edward Ryan McCall III, owner of this ranch and a few million other odds and ends."

"Oh. Another name. Wonderful. Good question about the harem," Lisa said, giving the word its Middle Eastern pronunciation—har*eem*. "I'll bet he has the answer. Why don't you ask him the next time he buys you a diamond bracelet?"

"Excuse me?"

"There you are, Susan," said another woman. "I thought I'd lost you to that silver-haired, silver-tongued devil."

Lisa turned and saw a tall, young, beautifully curved woman walking in from the front porch. Her skin was flawless, her eyes were like clear black crystal, and she was wearing a red silk jumpsuit that had Paris sewn into every expensive seam.

"My God," Lisa said, unconsciously echoing Susan. "He does have a harem?"

"Lassiter?" asked the black-eyed beauty. "Why, yes, I'm afraid so. But we forgive him. After all, there's only one of him and so many, many needy women."

"Not Lassiter—Rye. Ryan. Boss Mac. Edward Ryan McCall III," Lisa said.

"You left out Cindy's brother," said the brunette dryly.

"Who?"

"Cindy," Susan said, smiling, "introduce yourself to this little houri before she stabs you with one of those elegant ebony hair picks. Where did you get them, by the way?"

"In the Sudan, but they were trade items, not a local craft," Lisa said absently, not taking her eyes from the tall brunette. Next to her and Susan, Lisa felt like a short fence post wrapped in a second-hand rag.

I should have stayed in the meadow. I don't exist down here. Not really. Not the way these women do. My God, but they're beautiful. They belong. They're real. And I'm not. Not here, with all these people who know each other and Rye/ Boss Mac/Ryan/Edward Ryan McCall III.

"And the eye makeup came straight from Egypt, too, about three thousand years ago. The dress is a variation of the sari," Susan said, ticking off each item on her fingers, "and the shoes are Turkish. The eyes are right out of this world. The coloring is Scandinavian with that perfect Welsh complexion thrown in, and the body is beautifully proportioned, if a bit short. Heels would solve that problem. Why don't you wear them?"

"Susan is a former model who is now running

a fashion house. She doesn't mean to be rude,'' the other woman explained.

"*Moi?* Rude?" Susan said, lifting her perfectly shaped brows. "The ensemble is unusual but absolutely smashing. Is it rude to point out that the effect would be enhanced by heels? I'd offer mine, but you'd have to cut them in half. God, I'd kill for such delicate feet. And those eyes. Is your hair really platinum blonde, or did you cheat just the tiniest little bit?"

"Cheat?" Lisa asked, puzzled.

Susan groaned. "It's real. Quick, put her in a closet or none of the men will look at me."

Lisa blinked, too surprised at being envied by the tall, cinnamon-haired beauty to say anything.

"Let's start all over again," the brunette said, smiling. "I'm Cindy McCall, Ryan's sister." She laughed as Lisa's expressive face revealed her thoughts. "That look of relief is more flattering than a wolf whistle," Cindy said. "Not that I blame you. Competing for Ryan with Susan around would be more than enough trouble for anyone, without throwing an overbuilt brunette into the bargain. Unfortunately I'm afraid you're both out of the running for my brother. Ryan already has found someone and it's all very hush-hush. But there are other single men here, lots of good food, and I even saw some wine lurking at the bottom of the beer cooler. In short, there are more reasons to smile than to wail.''

Lisa closed her eyes and stifled her cry of disbelief as Cindy's words echoed silently. *Ryan already has found someone.*

"She doesn't believe you," Susan said. "Do you think she has a name, or did Tinkerbelle drop her off on the way to chase an alligator?''

"I think it was a crocodile,'' Cindy said.

Susan shrugged. "Either one makes great shoes. Ah, she's back. If we're very quiet, maybe she'll tell us her name.''

Lisa smiled wanly. "I'm Lisa Johansen.''

"Ah, I was right about the Scandinavian genes,'' Susan said triumphantly.

Lassiter suddenly appeared behind Susan. He bent slightly, said something only she could hear and was rewarded by a heightened sparkle in her eyes and an outstretched hand slipped into his.

"Bring her back before dawn," Cindy said, watching Lassiter and Susan leave.

"You have any particular day in mind?" asked Lassiter.

Cindy laughed and shook her head. Lisa looked closely but saw no jealousy or pain in Cindy's face.

"You don't care?" Lisa asked.

"Lassiter and Susan?" Cindy shrugged. "They're of legal age. I'd hoped that she might catch Ryan's eye, but there's no chance of that now that he's otherwise involved."

"Where is she n-now?" Lisa asked, stumbling over the last word.

"Who?"

"Rye's—Ryan's woman."

Cindy smiled oddly. "Do you know any place around here where they don't keep time?"

"What?"

"He told me that 'her name is Woman' and she 'lives in a place out of time.' He goes to her there. That's why I can't meet her. Too many clocks at the ranch."

Bittersweet tears burned behind Lisa's eyes when she realized that she was the one whom Rye had described to his sister—and he knew, too, that Lisa didn't exist down here. She existed only in the meadow, which knew no time, where a poor cowhand called Rye came to see her whenever he could.

"But I want to see them together," Cindy continued wistfully. "Even if it's only at second hand, I want to see what it's like to be wanted for yourself, not for your bank account."

Lisa heard both the yearning in Cindy's voice and the echoes of Rye's determination. *Once, just once in my life, I'm going to know what it is to be wanted as a man. Just a man called Rye.*

Lisa hadn't understood what he meant at that

time. She did now. She understood, and it hurt more than she would have believed possible. Not for herself, but for Rye. She loved him as he had always wanted to be loved, and he would never believe it, for he wasn't a cowhand called Rye. He was Edward Ryan McCall III, heir to too much money and too little love.

"Oh, look at that gorgeous baby," Cindy cried softly.

Lisa glanced over her shoulder and saw Jim holding a baby in his arms. The cowhand appeared both proud and a bit apprehensive at being left in sole charge of his son. Jim's expression changed to pure pride when he spotted Lisa and hurried over.

"There you are. Betsy told me to be sure to show off Buddy's new tooth."

The baby waved his fat fists and stared with huge blue eyes at Lisa. She smiled in delight. After an instant, Buddy smiled back. The new tooth gleamed in solitary splendor against the baby's healthy pink gums. One fist wobbled erratically, then found its target. Buddy gummed his fingers with juicy intensity.

"He's cuttin' another one, too," Jim said, his tone divided between pride and resignation. "Teething babies are 'bout as touchy as a rattler in the blind."

Cindy blinked. "Beg pardon?"

"A rattlesnake that just shed its skin can't see," Jim explained. "It'll strike at anything that moves. Rest of the time rattlers are pretty good-natured."

"If you say so," Cindy answered dubiously.

Buddy whimpered. Jim shifted him uneasily, much more at home with a rope or a saddle than his baby son. Buddy sensed that very clearly. His whimper became a full-fledged announcement of impending unhappiness. Jim looked stricken.

"May I?" Lisa asked, smiling and holding out her arms.

With a look of pure relief, Jim passed over the baby. "He's so durn little I'm always afraid I'll break him or something."

Lisa's laugh was as soft as her smile. Automatically she rocked Buddy slowly in her arms while she spoke to him in a low, gentle voice. His eyes fastened on the bright amethyst cloth draped over her head. Little fingers reached, connected and pulled. Cloth tumbled down and gathered around her shoulders like a shawl. The baby's attention immediately went from the cloth to the pale crown of her hair where the shell-inlaid ebony sticks glittered. With tiny hands he reached for the tantalizing ornaments, only to discover that his arms were much too short. His face reddened and clouded with frustration.

Before he could cry, Lisa plucked out both sticks, knowing that if she left one in place, that would be the one Buddy wanted. The baby gurgled and reached for the black sticks, only to be sidetracked by the rapidly unraveling cloud of Lisa's hair. Long strands slid downward slowly, then with greater speed, until everything was undone and her hair hung like a heavy silk curtain all the way to her hips.

"Oh, Miss Lisa, now he's gone and messed up your party hairdo. I'm sure sorry," Jim said, a stricken expression on his face.

"That's all right," she said softly. "Buddy's just like children everywhere. He loves things that are soft and shiny."

She tucked the ebony sticks into her bodice, picked up a handful of her own hair and began stroking the baby's cheeks with it until he laughed in delight, displaying both his new tooth and the reddened spot nearby where another tooth was attempting to break through.

"Sore gums, little man?" she murmured.

Gently Lisa rubbed her fingertip on the spot. Instantly Buddy grabbed her finger and began gumming and drooling in earnest, a blissful expression on his face. Laughing softly, rocking slowly, she hummed an intricate African lullaby to him, as lost to the outer world as the baby in her arms was.

Cindy stared, caught by the image of the baby sheltered within shimmering veils of Lisa's unbound hair. The slow movement of her body as she rocked sent light rippling the length of each silken strand, but as extraordinary as her hair was, it was not as astonishing as the wordless, elemental communication shared between herself and the child.

Her name is Woman and she lives in a place without time.

Cindy didn't know that she had whispered her thoughts aloud until she heard Rye's bleak voice beside her.

"Yes."

Lisa's head came up slowly. Rye looked into her eyes, afraid to see the very money hunger for which he was searching—and finding only darkness and violet mystery, the essential Lisa retreating from him, gliding away among the shadows of all that had not been said.

"Where'd Little Eddy run off to?" boomed a male voice from across the room.

"He's with me, Dad," Cindy said, turning to look over her shoulder.

"Well, drag him on over here! Betty Sue and Lynette didn't fly all the way out from Florida just to talk to an old man."

Rye set his jaw and turned to give his father the kind of bleak stare that would have stopped any other man in his tracks. The stare was met by Big Eddy's determined smile. Eddy put a hand on each woman's bell-shaped fanny and shooed them toward his son.

"There he is, girls, my oldest child and heir, the only person on the face of the earth who's more stubborn than yours truly. First gal that gives me a grandson will have more diamonds than she can hold in both little hands."

A wave of laughter rippled through the room.

"I begged him not to do this," Cindy whispered.

Rye grunted.

"Introduce him to Lisa," Cindy said quickly. "Maybe he'll get the picture."

"The only way he'll get the picture is when it's tattooed on his nose with a sledgehammer. You know something? I'm looking forward to it."

"Ryan, you can't!"

"The hell I can't."

"He's your father. Even worse, it won't do any good. He's so desperate for an Edward McCall IV that he's been trotting eager studs through *my* house lately."

"So that's why you dragged what's her name up here."

"Er...ah..."

Rye hissed a savage word as his father appeared two steps away, a well-developed brunette clasped in each hand.

Cindy closed her eyes, thought a fast prayer and

said quickly, "Hi, Dad. I'd like you to meet someone very special. Her name is Lisa Johansen and
she…she…" Cindy's voice died as she turned
around to draw Lisa forward.

No one was behind Cindy but Jim and the baby
son sleeping peacefully in his arms.

12

Though a full moon shone brilliantly, drenching the land in silver light, Rye didn't dare take the steep, rugged shortcut to the meadow. Instead he took the wagon road, following the single set of hoofprints that had been incised into earth still damp from a late-afternoon thundershower. He concentrated only on those hoofprints and let the rest of the world fade into nothingness. He didn't want to think about the shouting match he had had with his father in the barn, or about the shadows in Lisa's eyes, or about the anger and cold fear he had felt when he had turned and found her gone as though she had never existed, leaving not even a word for him, not a touch, nothing.

Summer isn't over, he thought fiercely. *She can't leave.*

Thin, windswept clouds rippled in sheer veils

across the face of the moon, softening its brilliance briefly before dissolving until only night and stars remained. Evergreen boughs sighed and moaned as their crowns were combed by transparent fingers of wind. It was the same everywhere he looked, bush or grass, tree or silver stream. The night itself was subtly restless, caught between heat and chill, breezes turning and twisting, returning and unraveling, never still, as though the air were seeking answers to unasked questions in the darkness that lay beneath the blind silver eye of the moon.

But the meadow was hushed, motionless except for the spectral stirring of aspen leaves whispering softly of summers come and gone. A horse's low nicker rippled through the night. Devil answered and trotted quickly toward the rope corral that had been strung among a grove of aspens.

The sound of hoofbeats brought Lisa upright in a tangle of sheets and blankets. She hadn't slept for more than a few moments since she had returned to the meadow. She had hoped that Rye would come to her after the dance, but she had been afraid that he wouldn't. Even now she didn't trust her own ears. She had wanted to hear hoofbeats coming into the meadow so much that she had heard them every time she drifted off to sleep, and then she had awakened with her heart hammering frantically and hoofbeats echoing only in her mind.

But this time the sounds were real.

She came to her feet in a rush and opened the cabin door. Aspen leaves shivered in slow motion, each languid rustle a whispered reminder of long hours spent sated beneath the sun. Her hair stirred in a vagrant breeze, shining as the aspen leaves shone, silver echoes of summer past.

"Lisa?"

She ran to him through the moonlight, unable to conceal her joy. He caught her in his arms, held her high and close, let her hair fall in moon-bright profusion around his shoulders. The heat of her tears on his skin shocked him.

"I was afraid you wouldn't come," she said again and again, smiling and crying and kissing him between words. "I was so afraid."

"Why did you leave?" he demanded, but her only answer came as tears and kisses and the fierce strength of her arms around his neck. "Baby," he whispered, shaken by emotions he couldn't name, feeling his eyes burn as hotly as her tears. "Baby, it's all right. Whatever it is, it's all right. I'm here…I'm here."

He carried her into the cabin and lay with her on the tangled blankets, never releasing her, his own anger and questions forgotten in his need to comfort her. After a long time the hot rain of tears slackened, as did the sobs that turned like knives in his heart.

"I'm s-sorry," Lisa said finally. "I was going to b-be like the aspens. They smile so brightly, always, no matter what, and suddenly I c-couldn't and I...I'm sorry."

Rye hushed her with gentle kisses brushed across her lips and tear-drenched eyelashes, and then he held her closer still, wrapping her hair around his shoulders, letting her presence sink into him like sunlight into the meadow. Slowly Lisa relaxed, absorbing him even as he was absorbing her. She became supple once more, her softness fitting perfectly against each muscular ridge of his body. He closed his eyes and held her, breathing in her fragrance, savoring her gentle weight and warmth until her breathing was even and deep once more. He felt the gentle kisses she pressed into his neck and he smiled, feeling as though a weight had been lifted from his heart.

"Ready to tell me what that was all about?" Rye murmured, rubbing his cheek against the cool silk of Lisa's hair.

She shook her head and looked at him through shining veils of hair, her eyes glowing with something close to desire and not far from tears.

"It's all right now," she said, nuzzling against

his cheek, breathing in the scent of him. "You're here."

"But what...?"

Rye felt the heat of Lisa's tongue gliding along the rim of his ear and forgot the question he had been trying to ask. His hands shifted subtly on her back, savoring rather than comforting her. The change was rewarded by a hot tongue thrusting into his ear.

"You're going to get into trouble doing that," he warned softly.

"I'd rather get into your shirt," she murmured, running her right hand delicately over his chest, lightly raking his nipple to attention.

His breath broke. "Let's compromise. How about my pants?"

She smiled and bit his ear with sensual precision. When she turned to capture his mouth he was waiting for her with a hungry smile. She teased him as he had once teased her, nuzzling lightly at his mouth, running her tongue along the sensitive inner surface of his lips until he could bear it no longer. He moved swiftly, trying to capture her mouth for the deep kiss he wanted so badly that he groaned when she eluded him.

"Come here," Rye said, his voice gritty, hungry.

Lisa's laughter was a soft rush of air against his

lips as she obeyed. She sought him in the warmth and heat of his own mouth, shivering violently as his taste swept across her tongue. The kiss deepened and then deepened again until it was the slow, sensual mating of mouths that she had learned from him.

And that was just one of the things he had taught her.

A tremor of anticipation shook Lisa at the thought of the many ways in which Rye had teased and pleasured her. She wanted to arouse and to satisfy him in those same ways, if he would allow her the freedom of his body. Would he mind being loved by her hands, her mouth? Would he sense in her touch all the things that she couldn't say, the meadow being transformed silently by frost, the aspens blazing their most beautiful smiles in the face of the certain loss of summer?

"Rye...?"

"Kiss me like that again," he said huskily, seeking Lisa's mouth even as he spoke. "No ending, no beginning, nothing but the two of us."

Lisa fitted her mouth to Rye's, seeking him as hungrily as he sought her, sinking into him while time hung suspended between the season of fire and the coming of ice. The kiss changed with each breath, now teasing, now consuming, always touching, sharing, growing until both of them could hold no more. But no sooner had the kiss ended than he pulled her mouth down to his once more with an urgency that could not be denied.

"Again," Rye whispered against Lisa's lips. "Don't stop, baby. I need you too much. When I looked for you at the ranch, you weren't there. *You weren't there.*"

Lisa heard all that Rye didn't say, his anger and his bafflement, his wordless rage that everything had changed before he had been ready for any change at all, frost-scattered light blinding his eyes, summer's end.

"I don't belong down there," Lisa whispered, kissing Rye between words, loving him, preventing him from saying any more. "I belong up here in a summer meadow with a man called Rye. Just a man called Rye...."

The slow, deep kiss Lisa gave Rye made him groan with the passion that had grown greater every time she had satisfied it. Beneath his clothes, his powerful body became hot, taut, gleaming with the same hunger that had his mouth seeking hers, finding, holding, drinking with a thirst that knew no end. Beneath her searching fingers, the buttons of his shirt opened and the cloth peeled away. He groaned with the first sweet touch of skin on skin, no clothes between, nothing but her warm hands caressing him, smoothing the way for her teeth and the hot tip of her tongue.

"Baby, come closer," Rye whispered, pulling Lisa across his body until her legs parted and she half sat, half lay on top of him. "I need your mouth. I need…"

Lisa felt the shudder that ran through him when she slid from his grasp, evading him until her teeth closed delicately on his tiny, erect nipples. Teasing him, hearing him groan, feeling his skin grow hotter with each of her caresses, excited her almost beyond bearing. She forgot everything except the man who was giving himself to her sensual explorations, watching her with eyes blazing hotter than a summer sun.

She smoothed her face from side to side on his hard chest while her hands kneaded from his shoulders to his waist. Her fingers slid beneath his waistband, searching blindly, stroking, caressing, nails raking lightly over hard bands of muscle until she could bear the restraints of cloth no longer. She reached for his belt buckle, her hands shaking, wanting him.

And then Lisa realized what she was doing. She looked up at Rye, silently asking him if he minded. The glittering passion in his eyes made fever burst in the pit of her stomach, drenching her with heat.

"What do you want?" he asked in a voice so deep, so caressing, it was like a kiss.

"To undress you."

"And then?" he asked, smiling.

"To…pleasure you," she whispered, biting her lower lip unconsciously, then licking the small marks. "If you don't mind?"

Lisa felt the lightning stroke of response that went through Rye, tightening his whole body.

"I always hoped that someday I'd die of your sweet, hungry mouth," he whispered.

She said his name, husky and low, a promise and a breathless cry of pleasure at the same time. He reached for her but she slid through his fingers again, down the length of his body, leaving his hands softly tangled in the silken ends of her long hair. Her hands closed around first one of his boots, then the other, then his socks, until there was only warm skin beneath her caressing fingers. Her fingers rubbed beneath the legs of his jeans, easing upward until his calves flexed against her palms. As hard as ebony, hotter than sunlight, the clenched power of his muscles both surprised and excited her.

Slowly she worked her fingers back down to his ankles once more, pricking his skin lightly with her nails, smiling when she felt his response. She rubbed her palms up the outside of his jeans, slowly savoring the power of his thighs, hesitating, then sweeping up past the hard evidence of his desire without touching it. He stifled a groan of protest and need and pleading, for he wanted only those caresses that were freely given to him, and she had been so very innocent when she first had come to his meadow.

This time there was no hesitation when Lisa touched Rye's belt buckle. She undid the clasp, reached for the row of steel buttons that fastened the fly, then paused, trying to control the shaking of her hands.

"You don't have to," Rye said softly. "You're still so innocent in many ways. I understand."

"Do you?" asked Lisa, shivering. "I want you, Rye. I want everything with you. I want it tonight. I want it...now."

Rye's indrawn breath made a ragged sound as Lisa's fingers slid into the openings between the warm steel buttons. He twisted slowly beneath her and then shuddered heavily at the first touch of her fingertips on his hard, naked flesh. When she realized how intensely he enjoyed her caresses, her own body quivered within the grip of the same fever that made him hot to her touch. The last of her hesitation vanished as heat shimmered and burst within her, transforming her. She unfastened each steel button with growing anticipation, freeing him for her soft hands and even softer cries of discovery.

"You make me feel like a present on Christmas morning," Rye said thickly, wanting to laugh and to groan with pleasure at the same time.

"You are a present," Lisa murmured, stroking the length of him with her fingertips. "You're wonderful...but still much too well wrapped," she added, smiling and plucking at his jeans.

"Finish the job," Rye offered, his voice breaking between laughter and a need so great that it was tearing him apart.

Lisa had no hesitation about undressing Rye this time, but she was reluctant to give up what she had already unwrapped, even if only for a few moments. Rye was just as reluctant to lose the exciting heat of Lisa's fingers. Slowly, with many heated distractions, the rest of his wrappings slid down his legs. Without looking away from him, she threw his clothes into the darkness that lay beyond the shaft of moonlight pouring through the open cabin door.

Then Lisa stepped into the darkness, vanishing. When she reappeared moments later, drenched in moonlight, she was as naked as Rye. As he looked at the hardened tips of her breasts and the pale triangle at the apex of her thighs, his breath came in with a harsh sound and went out as a husky sigh. The sounds were like a cat's tongue stroking her, hot and raspy at once.

"Where were we?" Lisa teased, but her glance was already traveling down the length of Rye's lean, powerful body stretched out on the blankets. "Yes, I remember now," she said, her voice catching. She knelt, letting her hair sweep over his nakedness in a caressing veil. "It was summer and the meadow was a clear golden bell that trembled when we did, ringing with our cries. There was no yesterday, no tomorrow, no you, no me, just sunlight and...this." She caught up a handful of her hair and leaned down to him, brushing his hot flesh with the cool silken strands, following each slow stroke with the even greater softness of her tongue. "Do you remember?"

Rye started to answer, but could not. Delicious pleasure racked him, stripping him of all but a need so fierce that his breath unraveled into broken groans. Each sound sent another rush of heat through Lisa, shaking her. Her fingers flexed into his buttocks and stroked his thighs, glorying in the depth and power of his clenched muscles, the fiery heat of his skin and the intense intimacy of exploring him so completely, hearing his response, feeling it, tasting it.

"Baby," he said thickly, "I don't know how much of this I can take before..."

The last word splintered into a hoarse sound of pleasure. The dry, cool caress of Lisa's hair sliding across his loins was a violent contrast to the moist heat of her mouth savoring him. He tried to speak again and could not, for he had no voice, he remembered no words, nothing existed but the ecstasy she brought to him. He abandoned himself to her hot, generous loving until he knew he must be inside her soon or die. He reached for her, only to be shaken by a wild surge of pleasure when he looked down and saw her pale hair veiling his body and simultaneously felt the heat of her intimate caress.

"Come here," Rye whispered. "Come here, baby. Let me love you."

Lisa heard the words and felt Rye's need in every hard fiber of his body. With a reluctance that nearly undid the last measure of his control, she released him from the sensual prison of her mouth. When his hands captured her nipples, she moaned softly. She hadn't known until that instant how much she needed his touch.

"Closer," Rye coaxed, caressing Lisa's breasts, urging her to slide up his body. "Yes, that's it, closer. Come to me. Closer. Come closer, baby. I want you," he said, slowly biting her inner thigh, kissing away the mark, glorying in the violent sensual shudder that went through her when he caressed her soft, incredibly sensitive flesh. "Yes, that's what I want," he said thickly. "I love the heat of you...the velvet fever.... Closer, baby. Closer, come closer...*yes*."

Lisa swayed and bit her lip against the force of the sensations ravishing her body. A low moan was ripped from her, but she didn't hear it. She was deep within an ecstasy that devoured her so sweetly, so fiercely, that she could not say when it began or whether it would ever end. Suspended within the hot triangle of his hands and his mouth, she wept and called his name while he repaid her sensual generosity many times over, sharing her pleasure even as she had shared his, until she could bear no more and begged to feel him inside her again.

Slowly, with a sensuous anticipation that made his eyes blaze, Rye lifted Lisa, easing her down his body until she could feel the hard length of his arousal seeking her. At the first touch of him parting her soft flesh, fever radiated out from the pit of her stomach, drenching her with rhythmic pulses of heat and pleasure. When he slid into her, she made a hoarse sound and moved her hips over him very slowly, abandoning herself to him and to the waves of ecstasy sweeping through her. He tried to hold back, but the feel of her satin convulsions was too exciting. His hands tightened on her waist as he buried himself fully within her, sinking deeply into the velvet fever, giving of himself again and again until finally the last, lingering pulse of ecstasy had been spent. Even then he held on to her, staying deep inside her, savoring every shift and hidden warmth of her body stretched out on his chest.

After a long time Lisa lifted her head. He made an inarticulate sound of protest and snuggled her close once more. She kissed the swell of his biceps, then licked the mist of sweat from his skin with languid deliberation. When she turned her head and nuzzled through chest hair to the flat nipple beneath, she felt him tighten inside her. The sensation was indescribable, as though whole networks of nerves were being brushed with gentle electricity.

Rye smiled when he felt the telltale softening of her body, as though she were trying to sink into him as deeply as he was in her.

"Look at me, baby."

Lisa looked up. The movement tightened her body as Rye had known it would. He smiled even as he felt his own body tightening in anticipation. He kissed her lips, felt the racing of her heart against his chest and saw the sudden, heavy-lidded intensity of her eyes as she felt the growing tension of his body.

"This time we'll take it slow," Rye said, his voice husky with the renewed thickening of his blood, "so slow you'll think you're dying."

She started to say something, but he was moving within her and nothing else was real to her. She clung to him, following him, holding the end of summer at bay with every touch, every soft cry, every dizzying race of ecstasy. Each shift of body against body, each caress given and doubly returned, each sensation shared and enjoyed, each one was a brilliant aspen leaf shimmering against an autumn sky. Moonlight and midnight blurred together until time was suspended, all beginnings and endings swept aside and forgotten, leaving only man and woman intertwined, neither knowing nor wanting to know where one ended and the other began.

Lisa awoke at the first brush of dawn on the high peaks. She memorized Rye's peaceful expression before she eased from the tangle of blankets and dressed without waking him. She put a few final items in the backpack, shrugged into it and silently walked out into the white dawn. Frost lay everywhere, glittering doubly through her tears, a chill so deep that even the midday sun would not be able to deny the changing of the seasons. Leaving shadow footprints in the white, she saddled the patient gelding and urged him out over the lip of the high meadow into the world beyond.

The raucous call of a whiskey jack pulled Rye from sleep. Eyes closed, he reached for Lisa and found only empty blankets. He went to the door, opened it and looked toward the campfire. The world was still white, frost scintillating with each shift of the breeze. There was no sign of Lisa, no smoke rising from the direction of the campfire, no invisible twists of flame warming the chilly air. He stared for a moment longer, feeling as though something about the camp had changed, deciding finally that it was just the different perspective that came from the mantle of frost.

"Lisa?"

No answering voice came lilting back to him through the meadow's silence.

"Lisa!"

Rye's call echoed and then silence returned, broken only by the empty rasping of a whiskey jack flying over the ice-rimmed meadow.

"Lisa!"

The meadow's chill penetrated, making Rye realize that he was naked and shivering. He turned back to the room and pulled on his clothes as hurriedly as they had been removed the night before, telling himself the whole time that nothing was wrong, Lisa was simply out in the meadow checking on the plants and she hadn't heard him, that was all.

"Damn," he muttered as he yanked on his boots, "I'm real tired of turning around and finding her gone. Once I get my hands on her again, she's going to find herself wearing a short leash. The meadow doesn't need her attention half as much as I do."

The memory of the previous night returned to Rye with a vividness that sent heat snaking through him, changing the fit of his jeans within the space of a few breaths. He cursed his unruly body even as he remembered the caressing heat of Lisa's mouth. He had never known a woman so sweet and yet so abandoned, wanting only him, taking nothing from him, asking nothing of him.

And he had given her just that. Nothing. Yet still she had run to him through the darkness, wanting him. Just him. A man called Rye.

Rye froze in the act of grabbing his jacket from the floor. The uneasiness that he had been trying to ignore since he had awakened without Lisa stabbed through him, and in its wake came questions he could no longer evade.

She wanted just a man called Rye. But I'm not just Rye. I'm Boss Mac, too, and Edward Ryan McCall III.

He wondered if that was why Lisa had cried last night—had she expected something from him? Yet she had asked for nothing. Not once. And when her tears had been spent, she had made love to him as though he had poured a river of diamonds into her hands.

Restlessly Rye went to the cabin door and looked out over the white expanse of meadow, seeking any sign that Lisa was out there. Only the aspens seemed alive, their yellow leaves more brilliant than a thousand smiles. Memory tantalized him, something that Lisa had said last night, something that he hadn't understood then and couldn't quite remember now, something about aspens and smiles. He raked the meadow with his narrow glance once more, then turned back to the cabin, trying to shake the apprehension that was seeping through him as surely as the cold.

"Might as well make coffee," he muttered to himself. "Whatever she's doing, she won't be long. It's cold out there and she doesn't have a decent jacket. Hell, she should have had the sense to take mine."

Even as Rye said it, he knew that Lisa would never have taken his jacket or even have thought of taking it. She was too accustomed to making do or doing without things that most people took for granted. Suddenly the idea of giving her a soft, warm jacket made him stop pacing and smile. The gift would be unexpected and all the more cherished for it. He would buy a jacket that matched her eyes, and laugh with her as he zipped her into it, making her snug and warm and protected against the worst cold that winter could deliver.

Still smiling, Rye went out to the campfire. Halfway there he stopped walking, feeling uneasiness crystallize like frost in his blood.

There was no fire ring beneath the frost, no grate, no soot-blackened pot, no tools laid out for quick use. It was as though Lisa had never built a campfire there, never warmed her hands there, never fed hungry men freshly made bread and strong coffee.

Rye spun and looked at the meadow, realizing too late what had been bothering him. There were no tracks in the pristine frost, no sign that Lisa had slipped through the fence to check on the plants without awakening him. He opened his mouth, trying to call Lisa's name, but nothing came out except a low sound of disbelief and denial.

She was gone.

Rye ran into the cabin, telling himself that he was wrong, she couldn't have left. He flung open the closet door—and saw not a single piece of clothing. Nothing remained of Lisa's. No backpack. No camera. No film. No log or seed packets.

Nothing but a creased brown paper bag that had been put on the farthest corner of the highest shelf and forgotten.

He stared at the bag for a long moment, remembering the last time he had seen it, remembering the hurt in Lisa's eyes when she had discovered his identity; and then she had taken the bag from his hands, telling him that it had been for a man called Rye, not for Boss Mac, who had no need of her gift.

Slowly Rye brought the abandoned gift out of the closet. He opened the worn bag, reached in and touched a fabric so fine that at first he thought it must be silk. He upended the sack, letting its contents slide into his hands.

Luminous gray cloth spilled over his skin in a cool caress. Tiny glints of blue and secret hints of green gleamed from the fabric with each shift of his fingers. He walked slowly to the sunlight streaming through the open cabin door and shook the cloth out. It became a man's shirt, which shimmered in his hands as though alive, a gray that held elusive hints of all colors, all tints, all moods. The fabric itself was such a fine weave that he could barely accept what his sense of touch told him; he was holding linen of unbelievably high quality.

He stroked the fabric very gently, as though it

were smoke that would vanish at the least disturbance. The surface of a button slid beneath his fingertip. The satin texture caught his attention, as did the subtle patterns within the button itself. Slowly he realized that he was looking at ivory or antler cut very carefully so as to use only the cream-colored parts. The same care was obvious in the collar, which had no puckering at the tips and whose stitches were almost invisibly small.

"Where on earth did she get this?" he whispered. "And how in hell did she afford it?"

Rye looked on the inner side of the neck where most shirts carried a label. There was none, but the workmanship was superior to anything he had ever seen. He opened the shirt and searched in the side seams, where the most exclusive designers often left their labels. Again, there was nothing to be seen but the incredible care with which the shirt had been made. Every seam was finished so that no cut edges were visible anywhere. The seams were smooth, flawless, ensuring that the fine cloth would hang perfectly.

Unbelieving, he went over each seam again, running his fingertips over the myriad stitches, telling himself that it couldn't be true, she couldn't have made this for him with nothing more than the few tools she carried in her backpack. She couldn't have cut buttons from antler and polished them with her own hands until each button felt like satin beneath his fingertip. She couldn't have spent hour after hour sitting cross-legged on the cabin floor, taking tiny stitches, smoothing the cloth, taking more stitches and then more until the light failed and she had to put the shirt away until the coming of tomorrow's sun. She simply couldn't have... and yet she had. And then she had found out who he was, and ridden off without even mentioning the gift that had taken so much care to create.

What's in the bag?

Nothing you need.

Rye closed his eyes for a moment, unable to endure the pain of the truth that he held in his hands, all questions answered except one, and that one was tearing him apart.

I was going to be like the aspens. They smile so brightly no matter what.

But she had wept...and then she had followed summer, leaving him alone.

Why did you leave?

I don't belong down there. I belong in a summer meadow with a man called Rye.

Last night he hadn't asked her what the words meant. This morning he was suddenly afraid that he knew. Summer was over, and she had discovered that the man called Rye had never existed outside of the timeless meadow.

The shirt slid caressingly over his hands, tangible proof of what he had been too blind to see. He had been protecting himself so fiercely that he had wounded her unbearably, and he hadn't known that, either. Until now.

What's in the bag?

Nothing you need.

Rye stared at the shirt until it was blurred by the wetness that ran down his cheeks in scalding silver streams. Slowly he removed his jacket and faded work shirt and put on the gift that Lisa had made for a penniless cowhand called Rye.

It fit him as she had. Perfectly.

Lisa reined the gelding onto the trail that led away from the wagon road. The trail led over High Pass and to the neighboring Leighton ranch. Nosy immediately decreased his pace to a kind of slow-motion walk. Lisa urged him with her voice and finally with her heels. Grudgingly the horse speeded up. The instant she relaxed, Nosy's feet slowly became glued to the ground again. He wanted to go back to the Rocking M's barn and he wasn't prepared to be gracious about going in any other direction. He shied at every shadow, dug in at every blind turn in the twisting trail and kept his ears back in a way that announced his bad temper to anyone with eyes.

"Look," Lisa said, glaring at the stubborn animal's flattened ears as Nosy balked again. "I know this isn't the way back to the ranch, but it's the trail I want to take."

"You sure about that?"

Her head snapped up. She stared in disbelief at the trail in front of her. Rye was sitting on Devil, watching her. The horse's black coat was gleaming with sweat and his nostrils were wide as he drank in great gulps of air. Bits of evergreen and aspen clung to unlikely parts of the bridle and saddle.

"How did you...?" Lisa's voice faded.

"Shortcut," Rye said succinctly.

"You shouldn't have come," she said, fighting not to cry. "I wanted you to remember me smiling...."

"I had to come. You left something important behind."

She watched helplessly as he unbuttoned his jacket. When she saw the luminous shirt she went pale.

"You d-don't understand," Lisa said painfully, giving up the uneven battle against tears. "I made th-that for a cowhand called Rye. B-but he doesn't exist outside the summer meadow. And neither do I."

"You're wrong. I'm very, very real, and so are you. Come here, little love."

The soft command made Lisa tremble. "I don't think…"

"Let me do the thinking," Rye said, his voice husky, coaxing. "Come closer, baby. Closer."

With an anguished sound she shut her eyes, unable to bear looking at him without touching him. He was so close, but he was forever beyond her reach.

With no warning he spurred Devil forward, leaned over and lifted Lisa from the saddle into his arms. He buried his face in her hair, making no attempt to conceal the tremors of emotion that ripped through him when her arms slowly came around his neck to hold him as tightly as he was holding her.

"Meadow or ranch house, summer or winter," he said, "Rye or Boss Mac or Edward Ryan McCall III, it doesn't matter. They all love you. I love you. I love you so much that I can't begin to tell you."

Rye kissed Lisa slowly, wanting to tell her how much he loved her, needed her, cherished her, but he had no words, only the warmth of his body and the tenderness of his kisses. He felt the sudden, hot glide of her tears over his lips and heard her love for him told in broken whispers. He held her close, knowing that he would never awaken alone in the meadow again.

They were married in the meadow, surrounded by the aspens' brilliant smiles. He wore the gift of her love that day, and on that same day of every year thereafter. Seasons came and went within the meadow, cycles of renewal and change, growth and harvest, the elemental rhythm of tribal time. The golden bell of the meadow rang with the laughter of their children and their children's children, and each of them discovered in the fullness of their lives what the aspens had always known.

The velvet fever known as love is bounded neither by seasons nor by place nor by time.

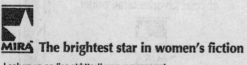

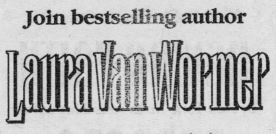